DOCTOR WHO
THE TRIAL OF A TIME LORD:
THE ULTIMATE FOE

DOCTOR WHO
THE TRIAL OF A TIME LORD:
THE ULTIMATE FOE

based on the BBC television series by Robert Holmes and Pip and Jane Baker
by arrangement with BBC Books, a division of BBC Enterprises Ltd

PIP AND JANE BAKER

Number 131 in the
Doctor Who Library

A TARGET BOOK
published by
the Paperback Division of
W. H. ALLEN & Co. Plc

A Target Book
Published in 1988
By the Paperback Division of
W. H. Allen & Co. Plc
44 Hill Street, London W1X 8LB

First published in Great Britain by
W. H. Allen & Co. Plc, 1988

The BBC producer of *The Ultimate Foe* was John Nathan-Turner
The director was Chris Clough
The role of the Doctor was played by Colin Baker

Printed and bound in Great Britain by
Anchor Brendon Ltd, Tiptree, Essex

ISBN 0 426 20329 1

Contents

Prologue

'The charge must now be genocide . . .'

Genocide!

The Doctor's face blanched, contrasting with his colourful patchwork coat. Snatched out of Time to stand trial for a crime of meddling in the affairs of other societies was traumatic enough, but the new charge echoing around the Court carried with it a greater penalty.

The ultimate punishment.

When a Time Lord is brought before the bar of justice, it is to no ordinary tribunal that he is transported. But then, as a member of the most remarkable species in Creation, this is only to be expected.

Plucked out of Time, the accused is incarcerated in a beam of turbulence which lances through the vast reaches of the four-dimensional Universe, to penetrate a unique dimension where all the processes of existence hitherto experienced are suspended.

Hovering in this singular vacuum is the venue for the Trial: a vast, incredible Space Station. Constructed like a baroque cathedral with dozens of thrusting spires and straddled with porticoes, the gargantuan hulk is embellished with a rococo scroll glorifying the achievements of the Time Lords.

In acknowledgment of the gravity of the proceedings a perpetual electric storm of Wagnerian magnitude leaps and dances with unabated fury.

★

This was the dramatic setting into which the Doctor had been pitched.

From the prisoner's rostrum, he watched events unfolding on the giant Matrix screen that dominated the Court. The Matrix contained the memories of all the Time Lords, and from there the black-garbed prosecutor, the Valeyard, had extracted two cases to present in evidence against the Doctor: interference on Ravolox, and aiding the brain transference travesty planned by the gruesome Sil.

Neither case caused him particular concern because of the strong submission he intended to offer in his own defence: the tale of the terrifying Vervoids; those plantoid creatures who had infested the intergalactic liner Hyperion III. Only his resourcefulness prevented the homicidal monsters from reaching Earth. His intervention saved the human race.

Having concluded his evidence, he awaited the Inquisitor's declaration of exoneration.

In vain.

It had been the Valeyard who spoke. 'Every Vervoid was destroyed by your ingenious ploy?'

Apparently a guileless question.

But the Doctor had realised where the vengeful prosecutor was leading. 'My Lady,' he said to the white-gowned Inquisitor. 'Had even a leaf survived and fallen on fertile soil, a Vervoid would have grown.'

No murmur of understanding came from the jury of his peers, the ancient Time Lords lining the rows of seats in the austere Court.

'The beings on planet Earth would have been eliminated!' he affirmed desperately.

To no avail.

The triumphant Valeyard had his victim by the tail and he intended to twist it! 'On his own submission,' pcrsisted the sonorous tones, 'the Doctor has admitted responsibility for destroying a complete species. Thus breaking Article Seven of Gallifreyan Law. For this there can only be one punishment!'

The Doctor knew what that was.

Death.

The forfeiture of all his remaining lives . . .

1

The Key of Rassilon

It seemed there was no help for the hapless Time Lord. Not a single witness who could speak in his defence.

Peri, his companion, was dead.

Mel, his subsequent companion, was somewhere in his future. He could call on neither of them to testify on his behalf.

Someone though – an unexpected and unlikely saviour – was waiting in the wings . . .

Two coffin-shaped caskets came drifting down a light beam. Like the TARDIS, which had been captured in a similar beam, they spun towards the hovering Space Station that housed the Courtroom, to land with a bump beside the deserted and somewhat battered navy-blue police box.

Both were occupied but the occupants were too dazed by the twisting, shaking and buffeting to do other than lie still.

Then a lid lifted.

A pair of crafty eyes peeked over the edge. Seeing nobody around, Sabalom Glitz oozed forth.

Sabalom Glitz! Thief, liar, and incorrigible rogue. A coward who would sell his grandmother to save his own skin. For whom profit was a god. A wheeler-dealer devoid of conscience, whom the Doctor had encountered on Ravolox.

'How the blazes did I get here?' muttered Glitz. 'And anyway, where in the Universe is here!'

He received no answer. The manipulator behind this

bizarre arrival was not ready to reveal his – or her –
presence.

Yet.

'Have you ought to offer in answer to the charge,
Doctor?' The Inquisitor's head, wreathed in a flattering
white headdress edged with a filigree trimming in gold,
inclined towards the bemused Doctor.

'Only one which you will not accept, My Lady.'

She knew what that was. The Doctor had been
claiming throughout the trial that the events displayed
on the Matrix screen were distorted.

'This so-called evidence is a farrago of distortion that
would have Ananias, Baron Munchhausen and other
famous liars blushing down to their very toenails! Many
happenings are not as I remember them!' insisted the
Doctor.

'It may not accord with your memory, Doctor, but –
as has been said before – it is possible for there to be
genuine differences in recollection.'

'Not that different. Even my story – offered in my
own defence – has been falsified!'

'Balderdash!' interjected the Valeyard.

A frown of reproval from the Inquisitor. 'If you wish
to make an observation, Valeyard, you will do so lucidly
and with due deference to this Court.'

'My apologies, ma'am. But I beg you to realise what is
being implied here,' came the obsequious rejoinder.

'I understand that without the use of expletives!
Doctor, what we have been watching on the Matrix
screen are hard facts drawn from the Matrix itself. And
the Matrix cannot lie.'

'With respect, if you'll believe that, you'll believe
anything!'

She adjusted the scarlet sash draped over her

shoulders, a gesture with which the Doctor had become familiar: an indication of a flutter of uncertainty. He decided to capitalise on the moment. 'I can quote an instance from my defence. According to what we saw on the Matrix screen, I destroyed the communications room on the Hyperion III. Never! I swear I went nowhere near that room. Why would I? By smashing the equipment, we were effectively cut off. Left to the mercy of the rampaging creatures whose sole aim was our annihilation!'

Murmurs and shuffles rippled along the benches as several venerable heads nodded in acceptance of the Doctor's reasoning.

'Fetch the Keeper,' ordered the inquisitor.

A uniformed guard quit the Court.

'Doctor, you are saying –'

'That the Matrix has been tampered with. Yes. That the ragbag of evidence you have seen is the result of perjury.'

Gasps of horror hissed: such an accusation was equivalent to sacrilege.

Indomitably the Doctor persisted. 'All I don't understand is who's doing the tampering. And why!'

He would find out.

Soon.

And from a most unexpected source.

Alone with only his fears for company, Glitz chose not to reveal his presence.

Not without a back-up anyway. His partner, and minder, Dibber was nowhere to be seen. And Glitz was no glory boy!

Quite the opposite.

He almost jumped out of his swarthy skin as a thump came from inside the other casket. He edged as far away

12

as possible: these monstrosities looked too much like coffins for his taste!

'Hey, what's going on?' came a shrill whine. More thumping from the inside. 'Let me out of here!'

'Dibber?' said Glitz. 'What's happened to your voice, lad –'

'I'm not Dibber!' declared the voice. 'Neither am I a lad!' Indeed Mel wasn't. Her mass of red curls emphasising the blue of her costume, the diminutive new companion rose from the second casket. 'And what's more,' she continued. 'There's nothing wrong with my voice!' Her brown eyes surveyed his hotchpotch apparel with disapproval. 'As a matter of total disinterest, who are you?' Half his size, a quarter his weight, Mel felt less fear of the blustering Glitz than he did of her.

'Er – I – er – Sabalom Glitz.'

'I'm Mel. You're shaking! Pull yourself together, man!'

'Well, I don't know where I am. It's very disconcerting for an experienced traveller such as myself to suddenly find he's somewhere he hadn't planned to go and . . .' A devastating thought! He gazed at the casket in horror. 'And arriving in a coff –' He could not complete the word. 'In a – Mel, you don't think I'm – I mean, I haven't been croaked, have I?'

Glitz was alive and kicking and, with his devotion to self preservation at any cost, he was likely to stay so for a good many years.

No such rosy future stretched before the Doctor.

The Keeper of the Matrix, having obeyed the summons, was dispassionately tightening the noose around the defendant's neck. 'My Lady, no one can enter the Matrix without the Key of Rassilon.' He tapped the huge key safely fastened to a chain looped across his chest.

'Is it at all possible for the data stored within the Matrix to be tampered with in any way?' The Inquisitor was anxious to be absolutely impartial.

'Quite impossible, My Lady.'

'By whom is the Key used?' asked the Doctor.

'Qualified people. For inspection. Once in a milennium perhaps, to replace a transducer.'

'Keys can be copied, you will agree.'

'The Key of Rassilon never leaves my possession,' avowed the Keeper, pressing the precious article to his bosom.

'Except when it is in the hands of these qualified people!' persisted the Doctor.

The Valeyard stretched to his full majestic height: the argument was beginning to swing in the prisoner's favour! 'This is a ridiculous allegation, My Lady. The Doctor is challenging the evidence of the Matrix on the grounds that it has been tampered with. A charge he is totally unable to substantiate.'

'That is accepted,' the Inquisitor replied. 'Wild accusations of malfeasance do not constitute a defence, Doctor.'

'The Matrix can be physically penetrated. The Keeper has admitted as much!' shouted the Doctor. 'And the evidence you have been shown is totally at variance with my own memory! Therefore it has been deliberately distorted!'

'And who would do such a thing – if it were possible?'

'Somebody who wants my head!' He pointed an accusing finger. 'Such as the Valeyard!'

He was right.

Though not entirely.

His head was certainly wanted – but not only by the Valeyard . . .

14

2

An Unwelcome Intruder

'Ouch! That hurt!'

Mel had given Glitz a hearty pinch to convince him he was still in the land of the living! It hadn't been easy to find an exposed spot, what with his leather cladding on one arm and thick protective cloth on the other, but she'd managed.

'If you're expecting an apology, forget it,' she said. 'Now, I'm going through that door. Coming or not?' Without awaiting a reply, she began mounting the steps to a closed portal.

'Are they all your sort here?' grumbled Glitz. Nevertheless, he followed: better to have this tiny harridan by his side than nobody at all!

'Let's find out, shall we – Listen!'

A voice, feminine, authoritative, could be heard from beyond the door. 'There is only one way to rebut the evidence of the Matrix, Doctor . . .'

'Doctor?' Mel gulped in surprise.

The voice continued '. . . to produce witnesses who can support your version of events. Can you do that?'

'Of course I can't! You know I can't!'

Mel's face lit up. That was indeed her cherished Time Lord. But who was the woman laying down the law?

'Then we must accept the Valeyard's evidence.' The well-modulated female tones again.

'My Lady, such witnesses as I might call are scattered all over the Universe. And all through Time. How can I find them now?'

Then came another voice. Oily. Vengeful. Mel took an immediate dislike.

'My Lady, the Doctor is blatantly lying. His sole defence against the charge seems to be this ridiculous –'

Mel had heard enough.

She pushed open the door and burst into the Trial Room. Close on her heels, ludicrously trying to hide behind the petite girl, scampered Sabalom Glitz.

Consternation from the assembled throng.

The Doctor was the first to recover.

'Mel! Glitz! How did you get here?'

A brief glance at the courtroom . . . and Glitz was immediately on the defensive! 'I was sent, wasn't I? Not my wish, mind you.'

'Same here.'

Mel harboured no such guilt complex. Nor was she concerned for herself. Simply for the Doctor – who was occupying the prisoner's podium.

'What're you doing in there, Doctor? Why are you on trial –?'

'Be silent!' The precipitate arrival made the usually calm Inquisitor tetchy: there was a protocol to Gallifreyan court proceedings, and the intervention of extraneous persons was not according to the book. 'Who sent you to this Court?'

Sheltered by Mel and spurred on by the Doctor's obvious dilemma, Glitz became quietly expansive. 'That's the beak, is it?' he whispered, giving a nudge and a wink. 'They all look the same. Carved out of something hard and nasty.'

'I should warn you my hearing is excellent!' rasped the Inquisitor.

Bravado melted. 'Uriah Heep' took over. 'Naturally I wasn't referring to you, your worshipfulness –'

'Your name, I take it, is Glitz.'

'Sabalom Glitz, your honouress, at your service –'

'You said you were sent here, Sabalom Glitz. By whom?'

Before he could answer, another voice, low, well-modulated, menacing, replied.

'By me, Madam.'

Every head turned to the back of the Courtroom.

There on the giant Matrix screen, a spectre of Nemesis, was the Doctor's most implacable antagonist.

The scales of justice had tilted . . .

And not in the defendant's favour . . .

3

Evil Intent

Seen in close-up on the Matrix screen, the regular features appeared even paler, the dark hair, beard and moustache even darker, the black-as-night velvet costume even blacker.

His brooding eyes surveyed the scene below him. 'By me, Madam,' he repeated, enjoying the consternation his intrusion had caused.

'This is entirely irregular!' reproved the Inquisitor, not in the least daunted by the apparition of evil. 'Who are you?'

'I am known as the Master. And, as you see, I speak to you from within the Matrix.' An expansive smile. 'Proof, if any be needed, that not only qualified people can enter here.'

'But – how –?' The Keeper's fingers grasped the Key hanging on its silver chain. 'You – you haven't the Key of Rassilon –'

The Master held up an identical model. 'I have a very good copy, Keeper.'

'Ah!'

'Exactly, Doctor. Just as you said – it is possible.' His gaze switched from the mortified Keeper to his hated enemy in the dock.

Bold blue eyes returned the gaze: the Doctor appreciated the irony of his adversary providing the proof of his contention that the Matrix had been in-filtrated.

None of this impressed the Inquisitor. 'Do you

18

realise you are imposing your presence on an official Court appointed by the High Council to consider the most serious –'

'Madam, I *know*!' he interrupted. The orders of the High Council meant nothing to him. He was a renegade Time Lord who had been exiled from Gallifrey. 'I have followed the trial with great interest. And amusement.' The cruel lips widened, the regular white teeth gleamed. 'But now I must intervene for the sake of justice.'

'Humbug! Take no notice of him!' the Doctor fumed, affronted by the hypocrisy. 'Justice! He doesn't know what justice is. He'd see me dead tomorrow.' Quite true. The Master's dedication to the Doctor's destruction was legendary.

'Gladly would I, Doctor.' The smile faded as the Master recalled, with bitterness, the last occasion on which they had met. It had been on that despicable planet Earth in the nineteenth century when the workers were running amok. In alliance with another renegade, the Rani, he had embarked on a campaign to destroy his *bête noire*.

The Doctor's thoughts were following the same train. Only his went further. At the end of that episode – an episode he christened 'The Mark Of The Rani' – the two renegades were sent spinning into space locked in the Rani's TARDIS. Hurtling, out of control, towards the far reaches beyond the Milky Way.

How, then, had the Master escaped?

'I can guess what you are wondering, Doctor,' came the unctuous tones. 'And before I dispose of you, I will assuage your curiosity. However, my present concern is to prevent you from forfeiting your remaining lives to the Valeyard.'

Forfeit his remaining lives? Mel gripped the Doctor's

arm in fear. She had so many questions: who was this creep? What had the Doctor done? How had she herself been brought here? Yes, that was an unexplained puzzle. One moment she'd been immersed in writing an experimental programme for one of the TARDIS's complex computers – the next she'd found herself incarcerated in a custom-made casket. No light. No sound. Until, lifting the lid, she was confronted by the shivering specimen now doing his best to wheedle past the guards and out of the door!

Futile. The guards, clad in immaculate uniforms of cream, red and gold, were not merely ceremonial adjuncts to the elegant assembly. Nor were the phasers they levelled loaded with blanks. Glitz, coward incarnate, hurriedly retreated to the dock, using the Doctor's portly form for a shield!

The Master was continuing. 'As an opponent, Doctor, I can deal with you.'

'What's he on about, Doctor –?'

'Sssh!' The Doctor wanted to hear what was being said.

'But . . . I am not prepared to countenance a rival.'

A rival? The Doctor was intrigued. 'To which rival do you refer –'

'My Lady,' the Valeyard cut in. 'I must propose an immediate adjournment.'

'I am sorry, Valeyard. The prosecution's evidence is completed. The ball, as the Doctor might say, is now out of your court.'

'Admirably put. I have little regard for the idiotic High Council, but in selecting you to preside over this travesty of a hearing, Madam, they chose wisely.' The Master's audacity left the Inquisitor speechless. He carried on talking. 'Doctor, I have sent you two star witnesses. I knew you would need them.'

'No!' the Valeyard thundered. Beneath his close-fitting skull-cap, his forehead creased into a scowl. 'With respect, My Lady, the matter of admissible witnesses is for you to decide. We have seen enough to know that Glitz is an admitted criminal.' He was referring to evidence presented at the beginning of the trial when Glitz had been shown on Ravolox trying to steal a black 'box' which he believed was priceless. No exaggeration. The 'box' contained the secrets of the Matrix!

'Any testimony from him, therefore,' maintained Valeyard, 'must be dubious in the extreme.'

'But not from me!' Mel averred. 'I'm no criminal. Nor am I a liar. Any testimony I give will be the truth and nothing but the truth.' She'd heard that phrase used in courtroom dramas and thought it would help emphasize her validity as an honest broker.

'We are not impugning your integrity.' The Inquisitor spared a smile for the earnest young Mel.

'Let Sabalom Glitz speak!' The clipped order was issued from the Matrix screen. 'I assure you, Madam, he is too scared in this august conclave to utter other than the truth.'

Hesitation from the Inquisitor: despite the unusual turn events had taken, it was her wish – and her duty – to ensure the Doctor had a fair trial. 'Criminals have been known to speak truthfully,' she said to the protesting prosecutor. 'Especially when their own interests are at stake.'

'My point, My Lady, is that this person who calls himself the Master, whoever he might be –'

A hoot of laughter burbled from the screen. '*Whoever* he might be!' The chortle rolled hollowly around the room.

Why did the statement afford the Master such

amusement, the Doctor wondered. As he studied the gloating face enlarged to many times its normal size, he felt a sense of foreboding that he could not explain.

But the mystery was about to be unravelled.

And when it was – the Doctor's presentiment of evil would prove to be only too justified . . .

Twelve-and-a-half

'This *person* . . .' re-emphasized the Valeyard, not allowing the Master's derision to divert him from his argument. 'Should not be permitted to produce surprise witnesses of whom the prosecution has no pre-knowledge.'

'As I understand it, Valeyard, the evidence for the prosecution is concluded. The Doctor may now, in his defence, call witnesses to rebut that evidence. After which you have the right to cross-question them on what they have said. That is the procedure.'

'If I might intercede –'

The Inquisitor had had enough interference from the interloper on the Matrix screen. 'You may not! You have no part in these proceedings, sir!'

'Corporeally, of course not. But I am present – and enjoying myself enormously.'

'I'm glad somebody is,' muttered Mel. 'The sooner this is over and we can get out of here, the better!'

'Maybe we could scarper together,' whispered Glitz. 'This has nothing to do with us now, has it? So why don't we make a silent strategic withdrawal? Just the two of us –'

If the expression in Mel's smouldering eyes was not sufficient answer for the thick-skinned Glitz, the Doctor's shove was. 'Quiet!' He was absorbed in the Master's dissertation.

'I merely wished, Madam, to comment on the shortness of the Valeyard's memory.'

'In what respect?'

'My Lady, pay no heed to –'

The Inquisitor waved the prosecutor's objection aside. 'Let him continue.'

'The Valeyard – or, as I have always known him – the Doctor . . .' A dramatic, deliberate pause.

Confusion rippled along the benches. Questions overlapped.

'What did he call him?'

'Did he say "The Doctor"?'

'Was that a Freudian slip?'

'Who was he talking about?'

Heads turned every whichway; the Inquisitor's regal halo, Glitz's close-cropped brown curls, Mel's mass of red ringlets.

'I don't get it,' grumbled Glitz.

'Doctor,' said Mel. 'Do you understand what's going on? I surely don't.'

'I wouldn't expect you to, Mel. I'm not certain I do myself.' How could he? The mind of the Master was a labyrinth so devious, Machiavelli himself would need a map! But the Doctor understood the renegade well. This was no slip. If he addressed the prosecutor as 'The Doctor', it was deliberate . . . He braced his shoulders, glared defiantly up at the grinning, oversized image, awaiting the explanation that he knew would come.

And fearing it.

'I repeat . . .' said the Master, '. . . the Valeyard is my most constant and determined of foes. And yet now he affects not to recognise me.'

'This is clearly a blatant attempt by the Doctor's cronies to fudge the issue,' blustered the Valeyard.

'I must admit to a feeling of bewilderment,' confessed the Inquisitor.

'Me, too,' added Mel.

24

'If the prosecutor's accusation of a deliberate con-
spiracy to deceive is true –'

'As it most assuredly is, My Lady –'

'Do not interrupt me, Valeyard!'

'I am merely fulfilling my function as prosecutor.'

'Then perform it in the accustomed manner. With
civility and decorum!'

'I stand corrected, My Lady.'

'Why not sit?' gleefully interceded the Master,
revelling in the disturbance he was causing in the
hitherto placid Court. 'After all, the dénouement was
no surprise to you!'

The comment deflated the Valeyard.

A heavy sigh from the Inquisitor: the prosecutor she
could control, but this smug interloper on the screen
was another matter . . . she returned to her theme. 'As I
was saying, Doctor, if the prosecutor's accusation is
true, I shall –'

'It's not!' A curt rejection by the Doctor.

'Then I fail to comprehend,' she retorted in exasper-
ation.

The Doctor ran a hand through his mop of fair hair,
wrestling with the import of the Master's declaration.

'No questions, Doctor?' The Master adopted a
velvety tone: the apocalyptic nature of the disclosure
was too delicious to be rushed.

'You – you called him by my name,' ventured the
Doctor.

'I did address the Valeyard so.'

Instinctively Mel drew closer to her mentor, sensing
he was about to be dreadfully wounded by the
revelation the sinister intruder was intent on imparting.

'Much as I hate you, Doctor,' asserted the Master. 'I
have never underestimated your intelligence. I believe
you know the substance of what I am implying – albeit

25

your conceits urge you to reject it.'

An accurate summary of the quandary ravaging the Doctor's hearts.

He wanted to hear no more.

To escape.

To shut out the cruel exposé about to be delivered.

But he couldn't.

'The Valeyard, Doctor, is your penultimate re-incarnation . . . Somewhere between your twelfth and thirteenth regeneration . . . and may I say, you do not improve with age . . !'

Treason

Shock had becalmed proceedings in the Court. Adorned with rigid hoods and caped robes of office, the venerable Time Lords might have been russet-coloured gargoyles poised on the rows of benches. The Inquisitor in her white, starched gown could have represented a statue sculpted from frozen snow.

'Can anyone believe that this worm, this lackey of the High Council, could be *me*!' The Doctor's voice broke the spell.

'Well you know, there is a similarity. When I clapped peepers on him, I thought – hang in there, Glitz, this Valeyard must be the Doc's brother.'

'Shut up, Glitz!' admonished Mel.

'Same shaped nose. And the mouth. He's got your mouth –'

'When you get back to wherever you come from, you want to have your eyes tested! He's nothing like the Doctor!' Mel elbowed Glitz aside and laid a comforting hand on the Doctor's arm.

The squabble did at least unfreeze the traumatised onlookers. The Inquisitor rubbed her brow wearily, trying to assimilate this extraordinary allegation. 'Frankly, I fail to see any relevance in this communication.'

'My Lady, these scandalous accusations –'

'Valeyard! The single purpose of this trial is to determine the guilt or otherwise of the prisoner on the basis of the evidence that has been submitted.' She turned to the Doctor. 'Examine your witnesses.'

Having been scathingly reprimanded by Mel, and convinced all this was of scant concern to him, Glitz in his usual predatory manner, had been scrutinising the panelling of the dock, sniffing out a possible profit. 'This is real machonite, y'know,' he confided to nobody in particular. 'Worth a few grotzis today.' The scent of money emboldened him. He approached the bench. 'Your honouress, I could give you a fair price for this little lot –'

'Glitz!' cautioned the Doctor.

'Carriage included . . . What?' The interrogative was addressed to the Doctor.

'You were sent here by the Master?'

'Well, he's a business partner, so to speak. We've pulled off a few tickles together –'

'The Court isn't interested in your squalid deals, Glitz!'

'Squalid, Doc? That's a bit strong for –'

'Quite,' interjected the Inquisitor. 'The witness will keep to the point.'

'Glitz, when we first met –'

'On Ravolox, Doc.'

'Yes. Your main interest was in getting possession of a chest of secrets.'

'Right. A black box.'

'What were those secrets?'

'I dunno. Scientific stuff, that's what he said.' He jerked a thumb at the Master on the screen. 'Stuff the Sleepers had been nicking from the Matrix for years, he said.'

'The Matrix!' protested the Keeper. 'My Matrix?'

'Right. The Sleepers had figured how to break into it. So they were creaming off all this hi-tech info to ship home to Andromeda.'

'Sleepers? Andromeda?' queried Mel.

'The constellation where they live, Mel. No more questions. Just listen quietly.' A difficult task for Mel! Playing the bystander did not suit her ebullient personality.

The Doctor resumed his cross-examination of Glitz. 'But they were operating from Earth?'

'Sure. That was their cover, wasn't it? They knew the Time Lords would trace the leak eventually.'

'My Lady!' The Valeyard sprang to his feet. 'This is a palpable tissue of lies!'

'I don't think so,' countered the Doctor. 'It begins to make good sense.'

Not to me, it doesn't, thought Mel, but she stayed mute in deference to the Doctor. No doubt he'd explain evenually. When the mood took him!

'Go on, Glitz. What happened then?'

'Well, Doc, it appears the Time Lords sussed out the leak and tried to knock off the thieving Sleepers. Used this magno – magno thing.'

'Magnotron?'

'That's it.'

'– which could only have been done by an order in High Council!'

A slow, congratulatory handclap from the screen. 'Of course, Doctor. These paragons of virtue, these peers of the Universe who set themselves up as Guardians of Gallifrey, simply drew the planet Earth millions of miles across Space in order to protect their precious secrets.'

'Causing the fireball which almost destroyed the planet!' The Doctor's chubby cheeks were flushed with anger.

Destroyed Earth, pondered Mel. How could that be? She'd come from Earth. Pease Pottage, Sussex,

England to be precise. And Earth was still there when she left! But then, she was a rookie in this game. The concept of Time Travel had her bemused. She glanced at her youthful looking mentor: who would dream he was over nine hundred years old . . .

'The destruction of your favourite planet was of little consequence in the High Council's planning, Doctor,' the Master continued. 'They needed to frustrate the recovery mission that was despatched from Andromeda. So, to ensure the mission should miss Earth and go plunging futilely into Space, the target was plucked from its orbit.' An extravagant gesture demonstrated this horrendous act. 'Thus saving Gallifreyan secrets.'

'And burning to a crisp all life on Earth!'

'Not entirely, Doctor. At the primary intimation of the coming holocaust, the Sleepers on Earth were able to set up a survival chamber.'

'But the High Council were unaware of that,' added the Doctor.

'Oh absolutely. They believed by renaming Earth and calling it Ravolox, it would become an insignificant interstellar speck lost among the myriads.'

'The sanctimonious gang of hypocrites were dishonourably covering their tracks!'

'Exactly. It needs a while, Doctor, but eventually you get there!' Sarcasm rather than approval: the Master would find it impossible to approve of anything his hated adversary did.

The Doctor was too infuriated at the enormity of the despicable enterprise to take up the cudgel. 'They put an ancient culture like Earth's to the sword for the sake of a few miserable, filthy, scientific advances!'

'Big market for them, Doc,' counselled the opportunist Glitz. 'So *he* said,' – indicating the Master –

'Worth a lot of grotzis he told me.'

'A lot of grotzis!' The Doctor's temper exploded. 'In all my wanderings through the Cosmos, I have battled against evil . . . against power-mad conspirators!'

A gracious bow from the Master – of amusement not acceptance of the insult.

'I should have stayed on Gallifrey!' The blue eyes shone with rage. 'The oldest civilisation – decadent, degenerate, and rotten to the core!'

'Gently, Doctor,' begged Mel, worried lest the passionate denouncement of the High Council alienate the Court.

'Daleks. Sontarans. Cybermen. They're still in the nursery compared to us Gallifreyans!' ranted the Doctor, regardless of the consequences. 'Ten million years of total power. That's what it requires to be wholly corrupt!'

'Doctor, these unseemly outbursts do not assist the Court,' admonished the Inquisitor.

'Nor your case,' urged Mel.

'Unseemly outbursts!' Nothing was going to stop the incensed Time Lord now. He had a full head of steam. 'If l hadn't visited Ravolox – as I then imagined it was called – the High Council would have kept this atrocity carefully buried –'

'Clever stuff, Doc, you've got to give them their due –'

'– as they apparently already had for several centuries!'

Stroking his beard, the Master enjoyed the fervid castigation of the Universe's elite. 'It pains me to make such an admission, but in this instance, I do agree with you.'

The renegade's support had a deeper, more sinister intent. He knew that earlier in the Trial, during the submission of the Doctor's adventures on Ravolox, a reference was made to the activities of the Sleepers, and the Valeyard had intervened to plead security of the State to have the evidence suppressed. Obviously, with the connivance of the elected High Council, he had perpetrated an ignoble cover-up. When the news of the unconstitutional deception reached Gallifrey, the authority of the rulers would be demolished . . .

'You have, Doctor, an –' the Master sought the appropriate epithet, '– shall we say – endearing – habit of blundering into things. And the High Council took full advantage of your blunder.'

'Explain that,' ordered the Inquisitor.

'You could ask him, Madam,' sneered the Master, signifying Valeyard. 'Those exalted culprits made a compact with the prosecutor to adjust the evidence.'

'Aha!' exclaimed the Doctor. 'I knew it!'

'In return for which he was promised the remainder of the Doctor's regenerations . . .'

'Doctor!' yelled Mel, interrupting the Master's explanation again. 'Watch the Valeyard!'

Having edged towards the door by which Mel and Glitz had entered, the prosecutor was now slipping from sight.

'Stop him, My Lady,' implored the Doctor.

'Do not fear, Doctor. There is no way he can escape.'

'That's true,' agreed Mel. 'The only door from there is this one.' She was a computer expert whose training and natural curiosity endowed her with an aptitude for accurate observation. Despite her uncomfortable arrival, she had noted that the corridor was a sealed unit.

The Doctor wasn't convinced. Experience during his trial had taught him to beware the wily Valeyard. He descended from the dock. 'Come on, Glitz!'

'What?'

'Move, man! He'll get away!'

'Yeah, but, she said there's no exit –'

'You want your money, don't you?'

'Money?' The effect was like magic. Glitz was through the door in a flash!

To no avail.

The corridor was deserted.

Somehow the Valeyard had escaped . . .

6

A World Apart

'Look, Doc, this is all too much for me. I mean, working a few shady deals is one thing, but disappearing acts – no thank you very –'

Ignoring Glitz's specious protests, the Doctor examined the walls of the enclosed corridor. 'There must be a way out of here.'

'There is.' The Keeper preceded Mel and the Inquisitor.

'Explain, Keeper.'

'The Seventh Door, My Lady. He obviously had a Key.'

'Which Seventh Door? Where?' The Doctor's search had been thorough.

The Keeper crossed to the wall. 'The Seventh entrance to the Matrix.' No trace of the entrance showed on the panel the Keeper indicated.

'Then open it!' shouted the Doctor. 'The Valeyard has to be brought back!'

'To fulfil that request would require an order from the High Council. I dare not –'

'Nonsense. Obtain such permission. The Court has many pertinent questions that it wishes to pose –'

Paying no heed to the Inquisitor, the Doctor snatched the Key from the Keeper and planted it, flat, against the surface of the wall.

The panel began to slide apart.

'You'll never find him!' protested the Keeper. 'The Matrix is a micro-universe –'

'Don't go! Please don't go!' begged Mel.

'I must. Perhaps nothing in my life has been more important than this, Mel. Come on, Glitz!' He hauled Glitz towards the opening.

'Who? Me?' protested the reprobate. 'Suppose I just wait here till you get back –'

A mighty yank – and Glitz, protests and all, was through the gap!

The panel glided shut . . .

Darkness.

And fog.

A solitary gas lamp spluttered and spat as it fought forlornly to illuminate the narrow alley, throwing into eerie relief the decaying Victorian setting.

Suddenly the night air was filled with drunken shouts and rowdy catcalls. Contrapuntally came a sweet chorus of children singing . . .

'London bridge is falling down . . .
Falling down . . . falling down . . .'

and then, dominating the cacophony, an echoing, evil laugh.

The Valeyard's . . .

A thin strip of intense white light accompanied by a high-pitched, electronic screech, sliced the darkness. A figure was ejected from its midst before the beam vanished: the Doctor.

'Not a pleasant journey. And rather an unpleasant place, don't you think, Glitz?' He turned to look at the spot where he had landed. 'Glitz? Where are you? Glitz!'

The sole reply was the mocking laugh. Swivelling in its direction, he caught a glimpse of the Valeyard. Momentarily. Swift-footed, he gave chase . . . but his quarry was swallowed by a dense patch of yellow fog.

Confused but undaunted, he began a cautious check

35

of the alley, pausing beside a large, full rainwater barrel. 'I can't believe you're in there,' he said, peering into the water – two powerful, gnarled hands broke the surface and, with enormous strength, grabbed the Doctor's neck!

'Glitz . . !' his cry was drowned by the water as his head was pulled, inexorably, down into the barrel . . .

Evil laughter. A gurgling shout. Glitz heard them both as he staggered from another shaft of white light. Despite entering the Seventh Door together, they had been conducted separately into the fantastic world of the Matrix.

'Doc?'

'Glitz!' came another gurgle. 'Help me, man! Help!'

Tentatively – and not relishing the role of knight-errant – Glitz sidled towards the plaintive cry. However, his guise of intrepid rescuer was shortlived. When he arrived at the combat zone, the Time Lord's head was out of the barrel and he was prostrated beside it.

'What's going on?'

'I don't know.' The Doctor struggled slowly to his feet. 'That is, I don't know if what happened was real or just an illusion.'

Since Glitz had not seen what happened, he didn't know either. The Doc did appear dishevelled, though. 'Someone's had a go at you, have they? Torn collar. That's real enough.'

'Would you mind?'

'What?'

'Feeling in the barrel.'

'It's full of water.'

'Is it?'

Glitz cupped his hands and scooped up the water, allowing it to trickle through his fingers. 'Okay?'

'Apparently. But whatever tried to throttle me just now was in that barrel.'

Quick as a flash, Glitz scooted aside. 'You're a fine one! I could've been attacked!'

'Unless – it was simply in my mind . . .' The Doctor shook his head. Not a droplet of water flicked from his curly mop.

'You're a weirdo, d'you know that? If it wasn't for the grotzis, you wouldn't see me for dust! As it is, I'm here under protest. Wherever, "here" is!'

' "*Here*" is inside the Matrix. We're not in the real world any longer.'

'How can we be in a different world? We stepped through a door, that's all.'

'Exactly. Into the Matrix. Where the only logic is that there is no logic!'

'I knew this was a mistake. Never wanted to come in the first place!' He rummaged in his pocket. 'My grip on reality isn't too good at the best of times.' He found what he was seeking – a rumpled sheet of paper. 'Grab hold. This is for you. Now, where's the quickest way out of –'

'It's a note from the Master!' exclaimed the Doctor after glancing at the note.

'I know that! I've just given it to you!' He squinted over the Doctor's shoulder. 'He said it would be useful.'

'Did he!'

' "The Fantasy Factory, proprietor J. J. Chambers", ' read Glitz.

'The Valeyard's base!'

'Yeah?'

'Has to be. Why else was I sent the information?' The Doctor set off into the gloom.

'Where're you going?'

'To find Mr J. J. Chambers.'

'I can't see no factory round here.'

'Neither can I. Come on, Glitz. Best foot forward.'

Glitz hesitated. Either he had to find his way out alone. Or dog the Doctor.

Discretion being the better part of valour, he tagged after the Time Lord. Jettisoning an article of faith he cherished, Sabalom Glitz wished he were back before the beak! Even that court room would be preferable to these threatening surroundings . . !

'In all my experience I have never before had to conclude a case in the absence of both the accused and the prosecutor.' The Inquisitor had resumed her seat in the Courtroom.

'One and the same person, Madam,' insisted the Master from the Matrix screen.

'Couldn't you switch him off or something?' said Mel. 'He gives me the creeps!'

'May I say you're a charming girl,' countered the Master, stroking his Vandyke beard.

'And may I remind you that this is a courtroom in which we are conducting a very serious trial!' The Inquisitor's anger subdued neither protagonist.

'How can you when you've no one to try!' Mel piped.

'Unless you try him – *them* as you would phrase it – *in absente reo*, Madam.'

The Inquisitor rounded on the Master. 'You continue to maintain this absurd notion? Can you prove it?'

'Indeed I can. I know them both. Intimately,' he affirmed.

'Look, Madam Inquisitor, I'm not meaning to be disrespectful and all that . . . I don't really know much about legal protocol . . . what I do know is the Doctor could be in danger and we're doing nothing to help!'

'Not *could be*, my dear young girl. *Is*!' chortled the

Master. 'As you will be privileged to see on this sacred screen. I intend to occupy it for relatively few moments more. I have business affairs that require my presence. Duty, as they say on your planet, calls . . !'

'You have become a material witness in this trial,' blustered the Inquisitor. 'I order you to remain.'

'Madam, you have no jurisdiction over me. However, since I am minded to remain a while longer, I am content to be debriefed – I believe that is the jargon.'

The Inquisitor adjusted her scarlet sash before commencing her cross-examination: it allowed pause to contain her growing sense of frustration. 'Assuming I accept what you contend regarding the Doctor, how much of the evidence we have seen was contrived?'

'For a lie to work, Madam, it must be shrouded in the truth. Therefore, most of what you saw was true.'

A sibilant murmur rustled along the benches as the august Time Lords digested this statement.

'It rests with us then, to discover which was truth and which falsehood?'

'Precisely. Although I could elaborate.'

'A fat lot of use that'd be!' retorted Mel. 'He'd twist the facts to fit his own convenience!'

'You have a delightfully blunt approach. Quite an abrasive personality. An unusual choice of companion for the quixotic Doctor.'

'Talking of companions . . .' the Inquisitor remarked. 'You could answer one question.'

'I am at your disposal, Madam. Briefly.'

'The young person – the girl who died. Was that true?' She was referring to Peri.

'Ah mmm . . . the pert Miss Perpugilliam Brown.'

'Yes.'

'That was clever of the Valeyard, exploiting the affection the Doctor had for her.' The Master was remembering the second case which the Valeyard had submitted. In it, Peri was captured and her body used to house the brain of an ailing alien monster.

To all intents, the Doctor had made little effort to save her.

In the Valeyard's version of events.

The Doctor, watching the tale unfold on the Matrix screen, had been devastated by his pretty companion's ghastly end.

'An exploitation of which the Valeyard took full advantage,' volunteered the Master. 'But then, of course, he would know exactly how the Doctor felt.'

'Do I gather the story was untrue?'

'Let us say, Madam, the ending was prejudicially falsified.'

'Then she lives?'

'She is a queen. Set up on high by that warmongering fool Ycarnos.'

Ycarnos was the leader of a marauding tribe whom Peri had encountered on Ravolox: a warrior of immense strength and size with an overwhelming personality to match. He had been attracted to the waif-like charmer and, by fair means or foul it would seem, had won her affections.

'I'm pleased.' The Inquisitor was genuinely relieved: the Doctor's distress at being party to Peri's demise had touched her.

Death meant nothing to the Master. 'Sentiment, Madam, has no place in a court of law. Nor will it keep the Doctor alive.'

Or Sabalom Glitz.

Who was at that moment walking into danger from which the Doctor would be powerless to save him . . .

40

7

A Lethal Greeting

Bright fairy-lights formed an arc above an illuminated sign –

'THE FANTASY FACTORY'

Splayed from the shimmering arc, twinkling, scintillating multicoloured bulbs were arranged to represent dazzling rays springing from a sun cut in half by the horizon.

Below this resplendent display was a balcony that framed a glazed and curtained door. From here, a flight of wooden stairs descended steeply to a courtyard.

Striding into the courtyard, the Doctor and Glitz were bathed in a rainbow hue.

'The domain of Mr J. J. Chambers presumably,' mused the Doctor. 'A puzzle, Glitz. Why should the Master help me?'

'I never asked. Minding other people's business is the best way of getting into shtook!'

'True.'

'But it isn't going to stop you, is it?'

'Quite right. Come on.'

'Where?'

'Inside, of course. I want you to meet my other self.'

'Not me. I've done my bit.' Glitz shuddered. 'Oooh! Feels just like someone's walking over my grave!' Hardly an original statement . . . but could it be a prophetic one . . ?

'Just pop in and say hallo,' the Doctor urged, making for the wooden stairs. 'You'll be perfectly safe.' Famous last words!

The glazed door was suddenly flung wide.

The sharp, arrow-shaped barb of a harpoon glinted in the whirligig of lights, before streaking, with lethal accuracy, for its target.

Glitz's scream rent the air . . . as the harpoon thudded into his chest . . .

The Master stared sardonically down from the screen: these minions were destined to be at his mercy – although they had yet to become acquainted with the fact. Revelling in his game of cat and mouse, he resumed baiting those present in the Court.

'Come, no more questions?'

Impotence was an intolerable condition for the Inquisitor. An able jurist with an incisive mind, she had been chosen from many candidates qualified to conduct this important enquiry. It was to have been the pinnacle of her career. The next step, a seat on the High Council. But the fiasco that was now unfolding would put an end to those ambitions.

'You've stayed remarkably silent, Keeper.' Failing to raise a response elsewhere, the Master switched his attack. 'Still wondering how I got hold of this?' Tauntingly, he held up the duplicate key.

The Keeper nervously caressed the genuine Key, but remained mute. What would unauthorised possession of the Key mean to him personally? Reproval? Castigation? And maybe worse! Suspicion that he had betrayed his solemn trust and been collaborating with the perpetrators of this heinous crime!

'You claim the High Council is behind the scheme?' The Inquisitor broke the silence.

'Indubitably,' he savoured every syllable. 'They set up this travesty of a trial, making a scapegoat of the

Doctor to conceal their own involvement.'

'Is there any reason why I should accept that allegation from a renegade Time Lord?'

'Yes. If your ultimate aim is to elicit the truth.'

Mel had stayed quiet long enough. 'Truth! Are you sure you know the meaning of the word!'

'What is it they say on your planet? Red hair denotes a temper?' he tormented.

'Ask him what his interest is in the matter,' she instructed the Inquisitor. 'Certainly not concern for the Doctor!'

'Oh indeed not, my fiery vixen. But the Doctor is well matched against himself. One must destroy the other.'

'It is beyond belief that an individual as evil could have begun his existence in the hallowed halls of Gallifrey.' The Inquisitor viewed the Master with distaste.

'You are naive, Madam.' Back to Mel. 'I think I would lay a shade of odds on the Valeyard. But the possibility of their mutual destruction must exist. That would be perfect.'

'Can't you stop him!' Mel rounded on the Inquisitor. 'Sitting here like stuffed dummies while the Doctor –'

'Be quiet, girl!' The Inquisitor turned to the Master. 'I find it difficult to accept that your sole motive for interfering was the base desire for revenge.'

'Madam, there is nothing purer and more unsullied than the desire for revenge. But if you follow the metaphor, I have thrown a pebble into the water, perhaps killing two birds with one stone, and causing ripples that will rock the High Council to its foundations. What more could a renegade wish for . . .?'

'Rock the High Council?'

'The High Council is impregnable!'

'He's speaking treason!'

The sages on the benches did not hide their scepticism.

'Have him arrested, Madam Inquisitor!' A hollow – cheeked veteran of two thousand years was completely carried away.

'One cannot arrest an image, Xeroniam,' said his neighbour, a mere juvenile of a thousand and eight.

Confusion reigned.

Dignity had evaporated from the proceedings.

'Why don't you clear off!' demanded Mel. 'The sooner you go, the sooner we can see what's happening to the Doctor and Glitz!'

'To do so will afford me great pleasure, my dear Melanie. Though I doubt you will enjoy the sight . . .'

Nor did she.

The Master's leering face faded.

The screen went white.

Then a dim outline came floating into the vacated space.

Fuzzy at first. Indeterminate . . .

It resolved itself into a figure. Lying flat. Unmoving.

Mel drew in her breath as the picture hardened . . . into a corpse-like body prone on the cobblestones.

She peered closer.

Fearful.

It was almost with a guilty sense of relief that she recognised not the Doctor but Glitz.

Relief gave way to a gasp of revulsion.

The petty crook was not resting . . .

He was skewered by a harpoon . . !

8

Mr Popplewick

The festive lights frolicked over Sabalom Glitz's waxen features, underscoring the sadness of the scene.

Sadness? 'You'll get cold lying there!' quipped the Doctor.

A pause . . . then the eyelids popped open. 'You're a hard man, you are. My nerves are in shreds. I could've been killed.'

'Not when you're wearing a Mark Seven Postidion Life Preserver!' The Doctor's insight into Glitz's character was unflawed by sentiment. Glitz was plump, but a layer of that plumpness was the concealed protective toggery he cannily wore: he was no daredevil; even his pyjamas were made of Attack Repulsor Polycreman pongee, fastened at the neck by Batayn Radaral Buttons with a fifty metre range.

'Yeah, well, whoever slung that thing hadn't sussed out my underwear, had they?' He examined the harpoon, gingerly testing the sharp point. 'So much for illusions!' He threw the offensive weapon aside. It clattered on the cobbles. 'What I don't get, is why me? I thought it was you he wanted to kill!'

'He's playing games. Wants to humiliate me.'

'Oh I see, he humiliates *you* by flinging harpoons at *me*! Makes a lot of sense, don't it?'

'Of course it does. By using fantasy and illusion, the Valeyard will try to destroy me.'

'Hang on. Take it more slow.'

'You're not that dimwitted, Glitz. No rapscallion of

your calibre could afford to be.'

'Yeah . . . well. I can see you would be confused. I mean, not knowing what's what. Real or unreal. But what I don't get, is where I fit in.'

'Your presence makes his task more difficult. He knows that. He also knows together we can fight him.'

'Fight!' The suggestion brought about a miraculous recovery. Glitz sprang to his feet. 'Look, I'm a small-time crook with small-time ambitions – one of which is to stay alive. I wish you very good luck, Doctor, but I'm off. I've done my bit.' He swaggered into the swirling fog.

'The Valeyard must be stopped. And his agreement with the High Council broken.'

'Something best achieved by another Time Lord.' Glitz's proposed departure was suffering somewhat from his inability to decide which way to go. Three paces east. A change of mind. Four paces west. Then south. Refusing to appear nonplussed, he sashayed in and out of the murk with diminishing confidence.

'Something that can only be done by me. And I'm seeking your help, Glitz.'

'Yeah – well – look. This is all mighty embarrassing.' It most decidedly was! He hadn't a clue how to leave! The north had proved no more promising!

'If you go – and I die – do you think you'll have a future? As the only witness to events here, the Valeyard will hunt you down . . . and kill you.'

Glitz's perambulations halted, abruptly. 'Kill . . ! Me . . ? You've got a mean method of arguing.'

'I'm simply assessing the situation.'

'Hunt me down, you reckon?'

'And finish you off! Now, hoist up your life preserver and let's get on with it!'

Glitz watched the Doctor mount the steps and open

the factory door.

Nothing amiss.

Still the sceptic, he picked up the harpoon before following at a jog trot . . .

The sole splash of colour in the fusty, cramped, Victorian office, was the Doctor's outfit.

All else was dark brown or grey. The mahogany desk complete with mahogany stool was reminiscent of Bob Cratchit's in the classic tale of 'Scrooge' by Charles Dickens.

An inkstand, copious ledger and old fashioned bell-push were dimly lit by a solitary flickering candle. So was the clerk busily scratching away with a quill pen.

Dressed in Victorian attire, fat, bespectacled and as drab as his surroundings, Mr Popplewick's assiduous application would have warmed the cockles of the aforesaid Ebenezer Scrooge's heart! He wavered not one jot when the Doctor advanced across the cramped room.

Nor did he glance up as the outside door opened again and Glitz eased in.

'This isn't what I expected,' Glitz whispered.

'The combination is a bit odd.' The Doctor made little attempt to moderate his tones. 'Hi-tech vistani alloy walls cocooning what appears to be rather a crusty Victorian clerk. Quite anachronistic.' He leaned over the desk. 'How d'you do? I think we're expected.'

The rotund Mr Popplewick continued his meticulous copperplate screed.

Glitz, remaining near the entrance in case he needed to beat a strategic retreat, nudged the Doctor with the harpoon. The sharp end!

'Ouch! Have a care!'

'Sorry.' He turned it round and nudged with the blunt end. 'Doc?'

'What?'

'Are you sure we're in the right place?'

'Perfectly.' He pounded on the bell. Repeatedly.

The moon-shaped face of Mr Popplewick was slowly lifted. 'Yes?'

'We've come to see the proprietor.'

'Do you have an appointment, sir? Mr Chambers only sees people by appointment. Most particular about appointments is our Mr Chambers.' The precise, clipped consonants complemented the pendantic tenor of the imformation.

'Yeah, but we don't want to jump the queue,' said Glitz piously. 'We'll come back when he's not busy –'

'I think you'll find we're expected,' the Doctor cut in.

'And your name, sir?'

'I'm known as the Doctor. And this is –'

'Anonymous! I'm travelling incognito –'

'– is Mr Sabalom Glitz.'

Lodging the quill pen behind his right ear, Popplewick consulted the appointments diary, running a stubby forefinger down a list of names.

Glitz inched closer to the Doctor – and to a vantage point from which to look over the list: you never knew what tickles you might chance on by reading someone else's correspondence! 'If this Valeyard wants you dead,' he muttered in a low voice. 'He's got a rum way of going about it.'

'I told you. It's called humiliation.' A loud, impatient sigh for the pedantic clerk's benefit. 'Can you hurry? We haven't got all day.'

'There are procedures to follow, sir. Necessary routines to be completed.' The search stopped: doing two things at once – talking and reading – were not attributes to which Popplewick aspired. 'Even when I have found your name, there are many forms to be inscribed before you may move on to the next stage of processing.'

Processing! The prospect sent shivers along Glitz's spine: isn't that what they did to ersatz cheese!

Popplewick sniffed. 'Processing is very important in this establishment.'

He eyed the Doctor with distaste: the yellow and black striped trousers, the patchwork coat, tartan waistcoat and pea-green watch chain filled him with disgust. But devotion to duty dictated he must act with civility. 'I'm sure even you can understand that such things cannot be rushed . . . sir.' He could not resist spitting out the obligatory polite form of address.

The Doctor's attention had strayed. Faintly discernible in the flickering flame was another door bearing a notice –

ENTRANCE BY APPOINTMENT ONLY

'Oh, I don't know. I've always been a bit of an iconoclast by nature.' The reply was cover to enable him to reach the door.

Popplewick had detected this. 'You cannot go in there, sir!' he said, alarmed. 'Not without an appointment!'

Too late.

The door creaked open.

And so did the Doctor's jaw . . .

In amazement . . .

9

A Sticky End

Another Mr Popplewick sat inside.

In an identical office.

At an identical desk. Except that his seniority was reflected in petty embellishments: two spluttering candles instead of one; a branched hatstand for his raglan coat; engraved lettering on the tome-like ledger.

And this Mr Popplewick reflected the similarity.

Same frock-coat, winged collar, and cravat as the other Mr Popplewick. The sole difference was in the spectacles perched on his nose. They were half-frame, enabling him to blink over the top of them at the newcomers.

'Ah, Doctor.' His manner, too, was slightly more friendly: though still weighted by the dogma of bureaucracy.

'At least you're expecting us.'

'We all are.'

'Your lookalike outside wasn't,' volunteered Glitz.

'He is the exception. As a very junior clerk, Mr Popplewick is not permitted to expect anyone, sir.'

'Hey, Doc,' Glitz nudged the Doctor familiarly. 'What's he talking about?'

'I think it's called bureaucracy.'

'I prefer to call it order, sir. And the holy writ of order is procedure. I'm sure you agree.' The mellifluous tones, so reminiscent of his junior, were directed at the rough and ready Glitz.

'Oh, yeah, of course.'

'For example, you wish to see the proprietor.'

'Not me! Him!'

Pausing only to allow the interjection to die, Popplewick patiently plodded on. 'Now the procedure is to make an appointment.'

'We're already expected,' reminded the Doctor.

'But the junior Mr Popplewick is not empowered to expect anyone.'

'Look, old mate, you knew we were coming. Why didn't you give him the nod?'

'And upset the procedure?' Fleetingly the bland expression showed shock. 'The junior Mr Popplewick has his pride too.'

The stifling tangle of red tape goaded Glitz. 'I don't understand any of this. Here we are, waiting to duck a terminal sandwich from the Valeyard, and this screed's –'

Mr Popplewick huffed at the disrespectful description!

'– going on about whether we've got an appointment or not!'

'Gently, Glitz.'

But Glitz was launched. 'He'll be wanting to examine our teeth next to see how old we are!'

'That only applies to horses.'

'Does this geezer know that!'

'Mr Popplewick.'

'Yes, Doctor?'

'Is there no way we can expedite the procedure?'

'Expedite?' The portly clerk pulled himself up to his full sitting height. He was tall. Surely as tall as the Doctor. 'I am a senior clerk, sir.' His ample chest rose and fell with outraged emotion beneath his spruce alpaca waistcoat. 'To me the procedure is sacrosanct.' He lifted his chin – chins – with pride. 'My work is a celebration of all that is perfect. Why speed perfection?'

'Because your proprietor wants me dead.'

'Ah.' A temporary hiatus only. 'It seems you have found the one little weakness in our procedure, sir.' Matter-of-factly, he adjusted his half-spectacles, pinched the bridge of his nose between plump finger and thumb . . . and then selected a document. 'Would you sign this, please?'

'What is it?'

'A consent form, sir.' He offered his quill pen. 'The corridors in this factory are long and dark. Should you unexpectedly die –'

The mention of death convulsed Glitz. The harpoon clattered to the floor.

'Do go on, Mr Popplewick,' urged the Doctor.

'Should you, as was afore stated, unexpectedly die, our blessed proprietor, Mr J. J. Chambers, insists that he inherits your remaining lives.'

'The Valeyard must be concerned the High Council may no longer be in a position to fulfil their side of the deal.'

'Don't sign anything, Doc! You're a dead man as soon as you put your monicker on there.'

'No choice, Sabalom. We are in the Valeyard's domain. He can kill me any time he likes. I'll sign my remaining lives over to Mr J. J. Chambers.' He accepted the proffered quill pen and wrote his signature with a flourish.

'Excellent. Thank you, sir.'

'Now can I see your proprietor?'

'The waiting room is that way.' Lodging the quill pen behind his left ear – as opposed to the right ear used by his junior *doppelganger* – Popplewick pointed to a door on the far side of the office labelled –

WAITING ROOM

'You will be summoned as soon as your signature has been verified.'

The Doctor crossed to the door.

'This is madness, Doc!'

'Not if it precipitates my meeting with the Valeyard.' He twisted the old fashioned brass handle and was projected into a most unusual waiting room . . .

Mud!

Vast stretches of it, lapped by a desultory sea and hemmed in by barren sand dunes.

'This is a very odd waiting room. Where are the hopelessly out-of-date magazines?' he quipped. Even at moments this bizarre, the Doctor's irrepressible humour did not desert him.

Glitz had though.

'Glitz!' he called, aware he was alone. 'Glitz!'

And received an answer.

But not from the amiable rogue.

Instead, a gloating laugh echoed through the troughs of the sandy hillocks.

'Valeyard!' The Doctor recognised the laugh. 'What've you done with Glitz?'

'Look to your own predicament, Doctor.' The threat in the resonant reply was only thinly disguised.

The Doctor swivelled round, seeking the direction from which danger would come, describing a three hundred-and-sixty degree circle with his keen eyes.

Danger, though, was not to come at that level.

It came from below.

From the gooey patch of beach on which he stood.

The mud began to bubble . . . and, thrusting from the lower depths – a slime-streaked hand broke the surface . . . and scrabbled for the Doctor's sneaker-clad feet . . !

'This is an illusion! I deny it!'

'Not this time,' the Valeyard's voice proclaimed.

As if in confirmation, another predatory hand poked through.

And another.

'This isn't happening!'

Two more hands joined the assault.

The beleagured Doctor tried to pull his feet from the sucking, burping quicksand – but a sixth hand emerged . . . and his leg was captured . . !

The obscene fingers locked firm.

'You are dead, Doctor,' shouted the Valeyard as the remaining disembodied hands grappled for their quarry.

'Not yet!' The denial was firm . . . but his attempts to release his ankles were proving unsuccessful.

He tried to kick them free.

The sinewy grip on them did not slacken.

If only he'd had his umbrella he could have beaten them off. Instead, all he could do was pummel at those vice-like fingers with his fists.

A mistake.

In bending, he lost his balance . . .

And fell flat on his back . . .

In the muddy pool of quicksand . . .

'Goodbye, Doctor,' Valeyard called.

Goodbye it seemed indeed. The Doctor's torso . . . neck . . . then curly head sank beneath the mucilaginous slime . . .

10

To Be Or Not To Be!

Where was Glitz?

Like the Doctor, he had passed through that office door. But fractionally after him. Sufficiently delayed to land in a different area of the dunes.

The bleak aspect appalled Glitz. Not a person in sight. Not a house. A tavern. Or a tree. Nowhere to hide . . .

Ever since he'd met this trouble-prone Time Lord he'd been 'up the creek without a paddle'! Chapter of disasters: lost his mate Dibber; been dumped in that worst of all places, a courtroom; and encountered a homicidal lunatic called Valeyard!

The Valeyard! The reminder of the vengeful prosecutor jolted him into action. Running across the dunes, he clambered, puffing and panting, to the crest of a mound – a vantage point from which he hoped to clap peepers on the Doctor.

He saw him all right.

At least, he saw his sneakers, his orange spats and the cuffs of his yellow and black trousers.

Waving.

Kicking.

Sticking out of a seething pool of mud! The rest of him – body and head – had already sunk . . .

'Doctor!' Glitz's plaintive wail floated on a melancholy wind. 'Doc – tor – r!'

Acting the Good Samaritan – or whatever the equivalent was in his quadrant of the galaxy – did not come naturally to Glitz. But those pathetically struggling limbs stirred what little heroism existed in his soul. Slithering in the soft sand, he floundered towards the submerging Doctor.

'Hang on! Don't give in!'

He grabbed the Doctor's ankles. Yanked hard – and toppled backwards!

Recovering, he became aware he was holding the orange spats!

His gaze transferred to the mud. No sign of the Doctor. Just a few burping air bubbles rupturing the slimy surface.

'What a way to go.' He stared mournfully at the gulping bog. 'All in all he wasn't a bad old codger. Honest, of course.' A definite impediment in this recidivist's book! 'But apart from that . . .' Using his sleeve as a duster, he brushed specks from the spats. 'Still, nobody's perfect.'

'And that's the clue,' boomed a sepulchral voice. 'Nobody is. Not even the Valeyard.'

Glitz slumped to his knees. Trembling. Clasping his palms together in supplication, he realised he was clutching the spats – and slung them from him as though in fear of contamination!

A single, regurgitating bubble devoured them . . .

'Oh Great Cosmic Protector of grafters and dissemblers, save me,' prayed Glitz. 'A voice from the grave!'

'No,' came the response. 'Merely a grave voice.' How the Doctor loved a pun! For it was he who answered.

Not from below the ground but from above it . . . his tall form levitating from the flats nearby. 'Bad joke. Then, everything here is a bad joke.'

Glitz, almost mesmerised by the apparition, gawped at the resurrected Doctor. 'But you – you –' he indicated the mud in which the Doctor had been interred.

Only there was no mud.

Just dry sand.

He squinted at the Doctor's fair curls, pink cheeks and brightly coloured coat. Despite their dunking, they were unbesmirched. 'No mud . . . yet I saw . . .' His inspection centred on the Doctor's feet. 'And your ankle armour . . .' Clean and unsoiled, the spats nestled comfortably beneath the unsullied trousers. 'I don't get it! I just don't get it! I *saw* you going down! Saw you! Tried to pull you out, but you were a goner for sure!'

'Oh do concentrate, Glitz. How often must I tell you we're not dealing with reality?'

'Why waste your breath on that simple-minded oaf?' The clipped, incisive rhetoric could only have one source . . .

His long black gown, its stiff cape collar edged with white, billowed about the Valeyard as he stood, a stark figure against the skyline. 'You cannot speak as if reality –'

The Doctor turned, but before he could locate him, the Valeyard had disappeared. Literally.

To reappear closer. On the opposite side. '– is a one dimensional concept,' he continued.

Again the Doctor turned. And Glitz. Again the vanishing act . . . and a reappearance. Nearby. To their right.

'Fortunately there is a reality that you and I can both agree on. The ultimate reality.'

'Death?' said the Doctor.

' "The undiscovered country from whose bourn," ' quoted the Valeyard, ' "no traveller returns." '

' "Puzzles the will" ' supplied the Doctor. '*Hamlet*. Act three. Scene one.'

A scowl of disapproval at his own failings wrinkled the Valeyard's features. 'I really must curb these urges!'

57

He smoothed his straight, dark hair now unfettered by the tight-fitting skull cap he wore in Court. 'I've no wish to be contaminated by your whims and idiosyncrasies.'

'Yes . . . quite,' agreed the Doctor absently. 'What I don't comprehend –' Another vanishing trick!

'Over there, Doc.' The black antagonist was on the left now. 'Slippery customer your other persona.'

The Doctor swung to his left. 'What I don't comprehend, is why you want me dead.' Second thoughts. 'No. No. Let me rephrase that.' Too late. The evanescent Valeyard had done it again!

Glitz spotted him. 'Top of the dune!'

'What I mean is,' shouted the Doctor. 'It would satisfy my curiosity to know why you should go to such extraordinary lengths to kill me.'

'Come now, Doctor. How else can I obtain my freedom? Operate as a complete entity, unshackled by your side of my existence?' Another disappearance . . . and reappearance on the Time Lord's right. 'Only by ridding myself of you and your misplaced morality, your constant crusading – your . . . your . . .' Passion clouded his mind, forcing him to grope for the correct expression.

'Idiotic honesty,' suggested Glitz, understanding the thesis since it was akin to his own.

'Oaf! Microbe!' stormed the Valeyard, looming above Glitz and hissing the epithets into his ear.

'Pardon me for trying to help!' Glitz dug a forefinger into the earhole as if to remove an offensive blob of wax. 'I'm neutral in this set-up, you know.' In case his neutrality was not recognised or honoured by this disparaging genie, Glitz moved resolutely behind the Doctor.

The Valeyard ignored him, returning his attention to his true victim. 'Only by releasing myself from the misguided maxims that you nurture, can I be free.'

'Sounds like Armageddon's beckoning you, Doc,' muttered Glitz when Valeyard was no longer to be seen.

'With you destroyed,' a distant declaration from far off, 'and unable to constrain me, and with unlimited access to the Matrix . . . there will be nothing beyond my reach!' A triumphant swirl – and he vanished completely.

Relief surged through Glitz's veins – until he saw the Doctor striding determinedly across the flats.

'Here, where're you off to now?'

'To trace the Valeyard.'

'But he was here!' This crazy world inside the Matrix was too much for Glitz: suffocating bodies that didn't suffocate; persons that appeared and disappeared like rabbits out of a magician's hat; gurgling green gunge that became dry, golden sand . . . Madness! If this was the way honest people carried on, thank goodness for crime!

'Illusion, Glitz,' said the Doctor, maintaining his trek. 'The shadow not the substance.' He pounded towards the shore. 'Of course, if you don't wish to come, you can always stay and build sandcastles. I'm sure if you think hard enough, you can conjure up a bucket and spade!'

'Tell you something,' called Glitz, reluctantly trailing in the rear. 'When you two meet face to face, five grotzis'll get you ten that Valeyard'll be first past the chequered flag!'

The Doctor came to a sudden halt – a thick, dense mist was rising from the sea . . .

'Hey, Doc, what's that?'

Tentatively the Doctor sniffed the air.

'Back pedal, Glitz!'

'Not another illusion?'

'Alas, no.'

Gathering momentum, the cloud was rolling inexorably towards them.

'Sea mist? Fog?'

'Asphyxiating nerve gas. This is in deadly earnest!'

'If you must make jokes – steal them. Your own are schlock. Most comedians do, you know.' He was whistling in the dark, hoping against hope the Doctor was wrong. 'Change a name here . . . a word there. Impossible to prove it'd ever been pinched –'

'Run!' Despite his tendency to plumpness, the Doctor raced across the sands.

So did Glitz: terror lending wings to his heels.

The cloud's progress accelerated.

'Run, man! Run!'

'What-d'you think-I'm doing?' complained Glitz, labouring in the shifting sand. 'Playing intergalactic hopscotch!'

In fact he could well have been. His progress was spasmodic. Every now and again he was pausing for breath, mouth wide as he gulped in air.

'Faster!' Despite having to negotiate the soft sands, the Doctor was covering much more ground. 'Faster, Glitz!'

Trying to comply, Glitz stumbled.

Lungs aching, gasping and spluttering, he attempted to get up . . .

'Can't . . . breathe . . . can't . . . no air . . . can't breathe . . .'

11

Out of the Frying Pan

'Come on! *Do* something! We can't just sit here! We've got to help him!'

Mel's impassioned pleading had a minuscule effect on the serried ranks of Time Lords. In unison they turned away from the Matrix screen where they had been watching disaster overtake the stumbling fugitives on the beach.

'The Doctor chose to enter the Matrix,' reproved the Inquisitor. 'We are not empowered to interfere.'

'You parade of suffed dummies! He needs help!'

On the screen, the Doctor, lugging the spluttering Glitz, was managing to stay ahead of the ruthlessly pursuing cloud . . . Just!

'He's a Time Lord! One of you!'

The Gallifreyans remained impassive, unyielding.

'Call yourselves a superior species! No human being would see another in such terrible danger and do nothing!'

'If I may, My Lady?' The Keeper awaited assent from the Inquisitor. It was bestowed. 'Young woman, you are applying logical thought to a situation that recognises no logic.'

Mel clattered from the witness box and bustled across the well of the Court. 'Give me the key to the Matrix! I'm going in there!'

'Return to your seat!' instructed the Inquisitor. 'In my Court you follow orders.'

'Not a chance,' blurted Mel, and dashed towards the

Keeper, making a grab for the Key.

Nipping aside, he stuck out his foot.

Mel tripped and sprawled, full length, on the floor . . .

Scattering pebbles, the Doctor tugged the retching Glitz down a shingle slope, gaining temporary respite from the advancing cloud of gas.

'Come in, Doctor . . .'

Blinking, the hard-pressed Time Lord rubbed smarting tears from his eyes. The summons came from a dilapidated beach hut.

'You'll be perfectly safe . . .'

Deciding it was Hobson's Choice, the Doctor bundled Glitz into the tar-stained hut – to be confronted not by rickety deck-chairs and sun-faded parasols . . . but the sophisticated control room of a TARDIS.

Blundering to the console, coughing and choking, the Doctor rested on the central control, sucking un-contaminated air into his burning lungs . . .

Then he registered the pulsating tab of a Chameleon Circuit . . .

A functioning Chameleon Circuit? His own was de-funct. The police box could not change its shape to meld with any surroundings, but this TARDIS could . . . A fact that prompted the Doctor to wonder whether he hadn't jumped out of the frying pan into the fire.

'I never thought I'd welcome the sight of you,' he stuttered between gasps.

'It will not happen again,' came the uncompromising rejoinder.

'What puzzles me – is why it's happening now.'

The muzziness induced by the gas was beginning to recede: self-preservation ousted relief, and he hastily put the bulk of the console between himself and his malignant host.

'The explanation is quite simple. I want the Valeyard eliminated. You are the most likely candidate to achieve that,' purred the Master.

'Hang on!' Glitz wheezed in the midst of a hacking cough. 'I don't get that! You told me – this flashy, fair-haired geezer was – the one you wanted to croak.'

'Silence, worm!'

But the truth was out. Glitz was exposed as the Master's lackey. A traitor. Sent to decoy the Doctor.

Being a traitor did not bother Glitz. There was even a degree of glamour attached to the status of a spy.

But to be called a 'worm'! Not on your life! 'Hey, show respect there! Nobody talks to Sabalom Glitz like that and gets away with it!'

Seizing the opportunity to exploit the split, and mindful of the maxim 'there's no honour among thieves', the Doctor fanned the embers of mistrust. 'Especially not a business partner. What was it, Glitz? A fifty-fifty arrangement? Or were you the forty-nine per cent?'

'Yeah, he's got a point.' Glitz rounded on the black-bearded renegade. 'Who voted you Chairman of the Board?'

The Master treated Glitz to a beatific smile. 'Sabalom. Sabalom. Remember our many fruitful collaborations. I beg you, friend, don't listen to him. Can you not perceive his motive?'

'The profit motive's all I'm interested in!'

'Naturally, Sabalom, old friend. And profit you shall have . . .' Condescension oozed. The ingratiating speech dropped an octave for the finale. '. . . after the Valeyard has been disposed of.'

Judging the sycophantic bartering to be concluded, the Doctor added his comment. 'Which completes the circumnavigational dissertation. Bringing us to my question. Why?'

'Am I aiding you?' The Master, evil though he was, had a handsome smile. He was enjoying the contretemps.

'Yes, why is the leopard changing his spots?'

'With you as my enemy, I always had the advantage.'

'Huh!'

'Oh yes. You are constrained by conscience. There are limits beyond which you will not trespass.'

'Constraints from which you've never suffered.'

'Thank you. I appreciate your magnanimity, Doctor, in conceding that.'

'The two of you'll be kissing and making up at this rate!'

'Perish the thought, Glitz!' groaned the Doctor.

'But the Valeyard, the distillation of all that is evil –' The Master almost smacked his lips as he uttered the word, '– in you, untainted by virtue a composite of your every dark thought, is a different proposition.'

Spelt out this precisely, the Doctor could no longer evade the import of the Valeyard. So far he had drawn a veil over the accusation, blotting it from his mind. Now he had to face the fact that the cold, calculating prosecutor was the personification of every deplorable act he had ever committed; every adverse deed he had even comtemplated. The malice he had learnt to govern had burst from its cage and been reincarnated into this monster known as the Valeyard.

'Additionally, the Valeyard has infuriated me by threatening to deny me the gratification of personally bringing about your destruction. And so, he must pay the price!' The Master grabbed Glitz and thrust him, unceremoniously, into the annex.

'Curtain speech? Or prologue to the next act?' The

Doctor mused. 'With the Master, one can never be certain.'

He tested both doors – to the exterior and the annex. His suspicions were confirmed. They were locked. And he was a prisoner. What abasement had the warped miscreant in store for him now . . ?

Commencing insidiously . . . vibrant, pulsating, variegated lights began to accost him . . .

They dipped and swirled . . . faster and faster, to the accompaniment of a staccato, supersonic screech . . .

He pressed his knuckles to his ears . . . twisted and turned in the accelerating strobic lights, trying to block out the brain-numbing assault . . . squeezed shut his eyelids . . .

The onslaught of the disorientating maelstrom would not be denied.

Gradually the clenched knuckles relaxed . . .

His arms fell leadenly to his sides . . .

The wrinkled eyelids slowly rose . . . exposing the blue eyes to the mesmeric lights . . .

Sight, hearing, muscles, senses, were immobilised.

The Doctor stood erect . . .

Unable to move . . . see . . . or speak . . .

A prisoner indeed . . .

12

The Baiter Bitten

Incongruously, the statuesque rigour of the Doctor reminded Mel of the waxworks in Madame Tussauds: a museum in London, England, that housed many effigies of the famous who peopled her planet Earth.

A shudder shook her slender frame, for it was the basement of the popular landmark that came to mind – the Chamber of Horrors!

She regarded with contempt the calm faces of the esteemed observers in the Courtroom. It was difficult to accept that these were the same species as the altruistic Doctor. Their impassivity was tantamount to callousness.

Her attention strayed to the Key of Rassilon hanging about the Keeper's neck. Her attempt to secure it had been baulked . . . would she have the opportunity to try again . . ?

The Master would have been arrogantly amused by Mel's futile attempts to gain the Key of Rassilon. Indeed, had he not been engaged in subjugating the Doctor, he could have told the tale of his own adroitness in obtaining access to the Matrix.

The Time Lords of Gallifrey had, over the aeons, developed a trait that could only be described as an acute case of Achilles Heel. These vain-glorious elitists no longer deigned to carry out those tedious day-to-day chores which occurred even in the most perfect of societies. Maintenance of the Matrix had been delegated – nay, relegated – to the Elzevirs, inhabitants of the Moon of Leptonica; a lunar satellite in the constellation of Daedalus.

These delicate creatures specialised in microtechnology and were, therefore, ideally suited to disburden the slothful Gallifreyans from the tedium of servicing and refurbishing the micro-circuitry of the Matrix.

This, then, was the Achilles Heel, the chink in the armour the Gallifreyans had unwittingly provided for the Master to exploit.

Unable to hypnotise a fellow Time Lord, he was under no such handicap when it came to the Elzevirs.

His mesmerising medallion easily enslaved Nilex, the supervisor of the repair team.

Symptoms of a fault were induced into the Matrix and Nilex, a vassal of the renegade, utilised the opportunity to make a duplicate Key of Rassilon for the Master . . .

Witnessing the Doctor's subjugation via a monitor screen in the annex of his control room, the Master grinned.

Satisfaction sent adrenalin pumping through his veins.

'No questions, Sabalom Glitz?'

'Plenty. It's the answers I can't unravel.'

He watched the Doctor's suffering with curiosity rather than concern.

'Would I be wrong in thinking the Doc'll soon be needing a machonite overcoat?'

'Nothing so crude. He's merely being reduced to a catatonic state.'

'Cata – what?'

'The violent assault on his senses will trip a defensive

67

mechanism. His brain will switch off.'

'He'll become a zombie, you mean?'

'Temporarily. Long enough for my purposes.' Jauntily he re-entered the control room, followed by Glitz.

An honorary fellow of the Universal Order of Sceptics, Glitz threw a punch that missed the Doctor by a whisker. 'Not a flicker. Nifty little trick. Have to teach it to me some time. Invaluable when I'm short of a few ready grotzis. Waltz into a bank, switch on the catatonic whatchermacallit – and, hey presto, help yourself!'

The Master was setting the Time and Space co-ordinates.

'We off somewhere?'

Glitz's partner did not condescend to reply as the dematerialisation bellow trumpeted . . .

A regal woman, ensconced on a throne, began to materialise in a cul-de-sac.

A crown could be seen perched atop the severe hair-style. A well-corseted bosom above virtuously volum-inous skirts. Using the Chameleon Circuit to con-vert his TARDIS into a marble sculpture of the English Queen Victoria, was a product of the Master's ir-reverent humour.

A segment of the plinth separated and the Master and Glitz, supporting the comatose Doctor, stepped from beneath the throne.

'This should prove an irresistible bait for the Vale-yard,' declared the Master, leading his supine victim through claustrophobic byways to position him, like a Judas goat, in mid-courtyard before the offices of Mr J. J. Chambers.

'So that's what you're up to!' exclaimed Glitz. 'You Time Lords take the cake! Talk about devious. I'm transparent as crystal compared with you lot!'

Ignoring the impertinent diatribe, the Master balanced the paralysed body, then sought cover in an adjacent alcove.

Pricked by an alien twinge of conscience, Glitz lingered to straighten the Doctor's crumpled pink velvet lapel. 'Poor old Doc . . .'

'Stop slobbering! Get over here!'

The squeaking of the Fantasy Factory door had Glitz scurrying for shelter!

Popplewick Junior, quill pen lodged behind his right ear, shuffled onto the balcony. He glanced down at the unmoving Doctor . . . and returned inside.

Cautioning Glitz to keep silent, the Master waited.

Mr Popplewick Senior, quill pen lodged behind his left ear, stepped onto the balcony. Peering over his half-rimmed spectacles, he tutted and returned inside.

Surreptitiously, the Master took out his Tissue Compression Eliminator . . . and held it ready to fire.

'Hey, you're not going to shoot the Doc, are you?'

'Be quiet!'

'Yeah, but –' Glitz wasn't too sure why he was protesting. Could it be a sneaking regard for the Time Lord? Or, more plausibly, was he squeamish at being an accessory to murder?

However, the TCE was not levelled at the courtyard. Its trajectory was higher. The balcony . . .

A rattle of the latch and the door opened.

But neither amply endowed crusty clerk exited.

Instead, the raven-black robed Valeyard strolled onto the balcony.

He did, nevertheless, share a common factor with the ponderous bureaucrats – a quill pen tucked behind his ear.

The Master triggered the TCE.

A lethal ray hit the Valeyard . . . Dead centre!

No effect. The ray was deflected.

Bemused, the Master fired again.

Same result.

'You really are a second rate adversary,' called the Valeyard. 'Did you imagine I'd be lured by such a transparent ploy?' He was referring to the Doctor who had remained transfixed throughout. 'Second-rate in the extreme!' He plucked the quill from behind his ear and lobbed it towards the alcove.

Startled, the Master recoiled into Glitz as the quill gently floated to the ground – and exploded with an eruption of flames!

In disarray, the erstwhile ambushers retreated, pursued by the Valeyard's mocking laughter.

Another quill exploded. The shockwave of acrid cordite buffeted them.

Dignity cast to the winds, the pair scarpered for dear life. Detonating quills strafed the cobblestones in a demonic blitzkrieg, forcing them to hop a zigzag course like demented Dervishes!

Echoing, almost manic, laughter completed their nightmare.

Diving into a narrow passageway, Glitz halted. Nursing a stitch in his side and restraining the Master, he recalled his experience on the dunes and the Doctor's confident explanation.

'Look, hang on, this could all be an illusion.'

'Then stay and find out!' The renegade fetched Glitz a clout that buckled him over, then made a dash for the nearby statue of Victoria.

Within seconds the stately queen dematerialised, taking the Master to safety.

Abandoned, winded, Glitz watched a quill float daintily to rest in front of him.

The explosion hurled him against the lichen-covered, crumbling wall, where he slumped; an inert heap . . .

Triumphant now, the mocking, laughter rang out . . . then faded . . . there was no one to hear.

No one able to hear, that was.

For Glitz was either unconscious or dead.

And the intended decoy still occupying centre stage, had had all his faculties numbed . . .

13

False Witness

'Doctor . . .' the piping call expired in a whisper.

'Doctor . . .' It seemed to be filtering from the sepulchral depths of an archway off the courtyard.

'Doctor . . .' The gentle summons was persuasive, caressing . . .

And was there a smidgen of movement from the Doctor's petrified body . . ? Had the Master's pernicious spell begun to lose its potency?

Stiff lips struggled to part, the larynx to create sound. 'M . . . M . . . M . . .'

'Doctor . . .'

'Mel?' Hoarse, muffled, nevertheless the name was clear.

'Where are you, Doctor?' A darting, indistinct silhouette could be vaguely glimpsed in the gloom of the archway.

'Mel?' He flexed his fingers, the rigidity abating.

'Doctor, is that you?' The ethereal shape took on more definition: tiny, slim, feminine.

'Yes. Yes. Of course it's me. Where are you?'

A graceful arm protruded from the shadows, beckoning. 'This way. Quickly!'

'How did you get into the Matrix?'

'Forget the questions! You're alive, that's all that matters. Now, please, follow me before it's too late!'

Spurred by the urgency in her tone, the Doctor ventured into the archway following in the wake of the flitting figure.

'Where are we going?'

'To get you out of this unholy mess!' She pressed against a dank, mouldering wall – an aperture widened . . .

Speculatively, the Doctor stepped through . . .

. . . And found himself confronted by two coffin-shaped caskets, and by the navy-blue TARDIS.

He was in the corridor of the Courtroom.

'Why have we come here?' he demanded of the sprightly redhead.

'Trust me,' she said. 'I know what I'm doing.'

'But, Mel, that's –'

'The Seventh Door.' She touched the wall where they had entered. The gap was no longer there.

'You're leading me to the Trial Room!'

'The Time Lords let me into the Matrix to find you. They hazarded a guess that I could persuade you to return.'

'Persuade me! Trick me into abandoning my pursuit of the Valeyard, you mean!'

'Doctor, you're not thinking rationally. You're too emotionally involved.'

'Who wouldn't be when confronted with the dark side of their psyche?'

'Don't you see that until you've cleared your name you're no better than the Valeyard? A renegade on the run. An outcast.' The bullying hectoring reinforced the sincere intent.

'Always the pragmatist, aren't you, Mel?' He tweaked the sleeve of her royal-blue blouse. 'But you're right, of course. Let's get on with it.'

'Doctor, you owe this Court an apology.' Thus did the Inquisitor greet the returning Time Lord.

'If I do, then it is unreservedly offered, My Lady.' A

glance towards the empty dais where the Valeyard should be, 'Although I still contend the prosecutor misled the Court.'

'We accept your allegation, also without reservation. Are you willing to take the stand again?'

'There will be no end to this affair otherwise.' He mounted the podium.

'The charge of genocide was based on your own evidence in relating the story of the Vervoids.'

'A charge refuted by the Doctor,' challenged his diminutive companion.

'It seems you have a champion in this young person.'

'I was there, remember,' asserted the champion.

What was it about the vehement response that caused the Doctor to pause . . . quizzically to study the pert, young face . . ?

'Would you accept her as an impartial witness? Or, at best, as not being your enemy?'

'My Lady . . . I would trust Mel with my life . . .' The solemnity with which the statement was pronounced was not typical of the Doctor. He spoke slowly, carefully, as if choosing each word advisedly.

'Then I think, for the purposes of this analysis, we should view again the destruction of the Vervoid creatures. Keeper?'

'My Lady?'

'Switch on the Matrix.'

> . . . A Vervoid appears on the screen. Head sculpted like a closed, ivory bud, it has sunken cheeks that project forward an O-shaped, rubbery mouth. Curling, transparent sepals shield ear-slits. Neither eyebrows nor lashes frame the lid-less, staring eyes in the grotesque, noseless face. A biped, its legs, body and arms are covered with waxy green leaves.

Mel's scream blasts from the screen as other tall, plantoid Vervoids complete a towering barrier about her, bent on puncturing her neck with a venomous thorn in their avowed and instinctive need to eliminate the human race.

'The Vionesium, Mel!' bawls the Doctor.

Jolted from her stupor, she fumbles with the catch on a golden capsule she is holding.

Abandoning cover, the Doctor flips open his capsule and lobs its contents into the midst of the Vervoids . . .

'Is this a true record of what occurred, Melanie?'

'What do I say, Doctor?' appealed the witness.

'Tell the truth.'

'Yes, but I don't want the Court to twist it like the Valeyard did.'

'The truth can't harm me.'

The scene was still continuing as she replied to the Inquisitor. 'That is what happened.'

. . . On the screen, bedazzled Vervoids try to shield their eyes from the flaring brilliant white light of the exploding Vionesium . . .

'Without the Doctor's inspired idea to use Vionesium, we'd all have finished up on the Vervoid's gruesome compost heap.'

Confirmation of her testimony was taking place on the screen.

. . . Disorientated, the creature's reel helplessly, moaning in pain: a danse macabre orchestrated by eerie uluations . . .

'Must we watch this again?' blurted the Doctor afflicted by sadness at the pathetic re-enactment.

The Inquisitor indicated to the Keeper to switch off before she spoke. 'Melanie . . . is it your contention that the Doctor was solely responsible for devising the scheme that destroyed the Vervoid race?'

'Absolutely,' the piping voice asserted. 'The rest of us were stymied.'

'A unique solution.'

'Out of this world!'

'An appropriate expression, wouldn't you say, my Lords?'

The elderly sages nodded, whispered comments affirmed their agreement.

'Appropriate?' Her voice was less bright now. 'Will someone please explain?'

'Young woman, Gallifreyans are uniquely gifted. They have no magic. A Time Lord's perceptions are of the highest order in the Universe.'

'All the more reason to admire them,' came the smart reply.

'It is also the reason they are subjected to special restraints. These talents should not be fecklessly exploited.'

'Feckless! If the Doctor hadn't used his precious talents to wipe out the Vervoids, I wouldn't be standing on this spot now!' Flushed with anger, she turned to the Doctor expecting him to speak up in his own defence.

He did not.

'Doctor, do you wish to question this witness?'

'No.'

'You have no evidence to offer in rebuttal?'

The Doctor shook his head. His melancholy resignation confused his young companion.

'Something's going wrong here,' she complained. 'I can sense it. You said the truth couldn't harm you . . . yet I've a feeling I'm attending a lynching party! Tell them you had no choice, Doctor!'

'There's always a choice,' came his sombre reply.

'Does your response mean you are prepared to accept

this young woman's evidence as a faithful represen-
tation of the facts?'

'Yes.'

The Inquisitor rose. 'In all my professional career, I
doubt if I have ever been confronted with a decision
more painful than the one I now have to make . . .
Doctor, you stand accused of genocide. The verdict
must be guilty. Your life is, therefore, forfeit.' She
gestured imperiously to the guards. Take him from the
Court!'

'Switch off! Switch it off!' cried Mel from another
Court. The real Court. 'The Doctor's been tricked!'

Indeed he had.

For the trial in which he was participating was bogus!

The power of the Matrix to foster illusion, had been
ingeniously marshalled by the Valeyard to hoax the
Doctor.

A masquerade which the genuine Court had been
watching on the Matrix screen . . .

14

Off With His Head

In the authentic Courtroom, the genuine participants watched the charade being enacted by their *doppelgangers* on the Matrix screen.

Two guards marched forward to arrest the Doctor.

'Leave him alone,' cried the bogus Mel. 'Don't go with them, Doctor.'

'Are you advocating I should reject the verdict?'

'At least plead mitigating circumstances.'

'I can't.'

'You must.'

'Remember you asked me once why I was prepared to take such terrible risks?'

Indeed she had – at least, the bona fide Mel had. This counterfeit of the Valeyard's looked a perfect outward copy of Mel, but she had not been blessed with Mel's extraordinary memory.

However – 'Yes' came the mendacious reply.

'I said then that unless we are willing to sacrifice our lives for the good of all, anarchy and evil will spread like the plague. The rule of law must prevail.' Quitting the podium, he stood before the Inquisitor. 'Madam, I accept your verdict.'

'Switch it off!' implored the real Mel again.

The Keeper complied.

'What are you made of? Stone?' she ubraided the

whole assembly. 'The Doctor's been tricked into be-
lieving that was *this* Court. The legitimate Trial Room!
An illusion concocted by the Valeyard to take advantage
of the Doctor's romantic nature! He's convinced he
must sacrifice himself. And you're content to let him!'

A lengthy speech for Mel . . . but she had used the
harangue to work her way nearer the Keeper . . . and
the exit . . .

'They are in the confines of the Matrix. We cannot
interfere,' reproved the Inquisitor.

'Well, I can!'

Prepared for the Keeper to trip her as before, Mel
stamped on his foot, snatched the Key from its chain,
and nipped through the exit!

The conquest of temporal physics that enabled Time
Lords to manipulate relative dimensions within their
TARDISes, had led to a transcendent refinement: the
micro-physical world of the Matrix. A world where the
memories and knowledge of every Time Lord were
stored: a communal, eternal brain. And, as with that
organ, it could regurgitate data in a sequential fashion
or a dream-like mix that defied cogent apprehension.

In seeking to enter this forbidden territory, Mel was
stepping into a kaleidoscope of reality and hal-
lucination.

Plucked from the sealed corridor by an Astanaeus
beam of light evolved from Thydostanic Kinesectoral
energy, she was sent pirouetting out of Time and Logic,
to be dumped in the decrepit locale where the Doctor
had been deposited.

Children's voices sang –

> 'London Bridge is falling down . . .
> Falling down . . .'

Lingering only to get her bearings in the badly lit

79

Victorian alley, Mel embarked on her zestful search for the Doctor.

He, at that moment, was being escorted aboard a tumbril ready to be transported to the place of his decapitation.

This gruesome prospect did not deter the Doctor from approving the style shown by his peers: he was to be conveyed to his execution in a manner befitting an Aristo.

The first guard steadied the shafts of the two wheeled death cart, while the second bolted the rear flap. A flick on the hind quarters of the chestnut shire horse . . . and the final journey began.

Clip-clop. Clip-clop.

The metallic clatter of the shire's hoofs initiated a swelling murmur of blood-thirsty taunts.

'Kill him!'

'Off with his head!'

'Bring the scoundrel to Madame Guillotine!'

'Death to the upstart!'

'Villain! Villain! Breathe your last!'

Mel's efforts to navigate the rat-infested warren of alleys were not meeting with much success. Concern for her own safety as well as the Doctor's was now a consideration. If Jack the Ripper had pounced from the gloom, she would have been terrified but not surprised.

So it was with relief she heard the raucous taunts and sped towards them . . .

'Off with his head!'

'Death to the upstart!'

Rotting cabbages and squashy tomatoes pelted the Doctor.

Jolting over cobblestones, the tumbril lumbered

through narrow streets of soot-grimed slums; the natural habitat for the pox-scarred, unwashed denizens shying their putrid garbage and baying for the Doctor's death. His arrogant stance and disdainful mien incited them to fever-pitch.

Into this mêlée thrust the diminutive Mel.

Gagging at the malodorous stench given off by the mob, she pummelled to where she judged the Doctor to be.

Slick as a razor, the upraised guillotine glistened, awaiting the release that would allow it to despatch its victim into the abyss, or, more prosaically, his head into the basket!

The tumbril had halted in the shadow of the keen-edged blade.

Erect, betraying not a hint of fear, the Doctor was reminded of the fine prose that brought *A Tale Of Two Cities* to a noble climax. The last speech uttered by Dickens' hero before he kept his assignation with Madame Guillotine.

' "It is a far, far better thing that I do, than I have ever done;" ' quoted the Doctor in rich, melodious tones. ' ". . . it is a far, far better rest that I go to than I have ever known." '

During this peroration, Mel emerged from the motley crowd. 'Never mind the Sidney Carton heroics! You're not signing on as a martyr yet!'

'Go away!' whispered the Doctor urgently. 'Go away, Mel!'

Mel did not move.

'That trial was an illusion!' she declared.

Illusion?

As her proclamation hit the air – everything happened at once.

The guards vanished.

So did the horse.

And the tumbril causing the Doctor to plummet to the ground in an undignified heap!

'You've ruined everything!' he grumbled, dusting off his stain-free jacket.

Stain-free?

Not only were the Doctor's clothes wiped clean, so, too, was the courtyard.

Gone were the stinking vegetables . . . the brutish rabble . . . and the guillotine.

'Ruined?' Mel was nonplussed. 'I've just saved your life!'

'All you've done is keep me from a confrontation with the Valeyard!'

'But you were on your way to –'

'– a rendezvous with death as a result of a bogus trial and my noble act of self sacrifice.'

'You knew it was an illusion?' said Mel disbelievingly. 'How come?'

Had she really been paying attention to the trial when it was being played on the Matrix screen, she would have known.

Or should have.

She repeated the question. 'How come?'

Then came the surprising answer. 'Through you, Mel.'

'Through me!'

'Yes!' His voice soared to a shout that reverberated around the enclosed courtyard. 'In your evidence at the bogus trial, you testified that you heard me deny the charge of genocide. You were never there, Mel. You'd never been inside the Trial Room at that time!'

He circled, ensuring that no nook or cranny should miss his words. 'With your extraordinary ability for total recall, you wouldn't make such an elementary mistake!'

'Okay, okay, I'm not deaf!'

'The Valeyard overestimates his own cleverness,' he continued, even louder. 'Like all megalomaniacs, he's consumed with his own vanity!'

He lowered his voice to normal level. 'That should've inflamed his bloated ego!'

He patted Mel reassuringly. 'Didn't you notice that once your stand-in made the false claim, I never again called her Mel? A clue you should have spotted! Come on!'

'Where?'

'To visit Mr J. J. Chambers.' He mounted the stairs to the Fantasy Factory.

'Who's Mr J. J. Chambers?'

Lit by the fluctuating lights of the colourful sign, Mel stood fast. 'I asked you a question!'

The Doctor smiled. 'You'll find out . . .'

15

Mesmeric Riches

'Sabalom Glitz,' Queen Victoria called.

At least, that was how it seemed to Glitz as he re-covered consciousness; lost when the exploding quill flung him against the wall.

'This way!' The imperious monarch's summons would brook no delay. 'Hurry, Sabalom Glitz.'

Glitz crawled forward . . . then regained his compos mentis. 'Oh, so you've decided to come back for me, have you?'

Like the Doctor, Glitz was only too aware of the maxim 'there's no honour among thieves'. It originated on the planet Earth, but held good for the pan-galactic brotherhood of which he was a founder member.

'Trust me,' the Master had urged when unfolding his plans to Glitz at their inaugural encounter. 'Trust me?' In Glitz's lore, this reassurance was practically a pass-word: identification of a consummate liar. He'd used the pledge frequently. Especially when dealing with the innocents abroad who believed in honesty. They'd 'trusted' him often enough.

And paid for the privilege!

He had no delusions, therefore, about the calibre of the partner to whom he was allied. At least, no delusions about his crookedness.

But he hadn't anticipated desertion.

'Did you entertain, for the briefest of moments, I would desert you, Sabalom?' Could the Master thought-read? He'd even picked up the same vocabulary!

'You cleared off, didn't you? Left me for dead, didn't you?'

'My friend, you wrong me. It was ever my intention to return.'

'Yeah? You could've fooled me!'

No onerous task mused the Master . . . but he resisted expressing the insult aloud. He had other uses for the cretinous rascal. 'Then, why am I here? Waiting to welcome you into my TARDIS?'

'I dunno. Haven't worked that out yet. My cerebral juices must've taken a shaking.'

'Your "cerebral juices" as you term them, will not be required for the task I have in mind.'

'What task?' said Glitz, sidling warily into the TARDIS.

'I want you to rejoin the Doctor.'

'When did I volunteer to become a permanent agent provocateur?'

'Sabalom, you underestimate yourself. Talent should be recognised. You are a maestro as a double agent. You have a vocation for it, my friend.'

'I've a nose for a con, too!'

'Such accusations offend my sensibilities.'

'Do they!'

Unappeased, Glitz joined the Master at the monitor screen where he was watching the Doctor and Mel entering the Fantasy Factory.

Entering the Fantasy Factory!

That was the last straw!

'If all that guff means you want me to go in there – not a chance!'

'Come, come, my friend. Collaboration between you and I is an essential ingredient of our plans.'

'You won't get me going near no quill pens again!

And that's final!'

A scowl distorted the Master's smooth forehead. Murderous wrath was never far below the surface and this idiot was driving his patience to the limit!

If he didn't need him . . .

But he did. To get back inside that Fantasy Factory. And if he wouldn't do so voluntarily . . . there was an obvious answer for a practitioner in the hypnotic arts.

The renegade reached inside his jacket and eased out a bejewelled medallion.

'Look at this, Sabalom.'

He dangled the fascinating stone temptingly before the cowardly minion's avaricious gaze.

'Yeah! Final!' The blustering wasn't ended. 'I'm not going! I'm staying here till –'

Glowing . . . the medallion began to swing . . . mesmerically . . .

'– I can get back to my –'

Two greedy eyes followed each swing . . .

'– own kind – and –'

Left, right . . . left, right . . .

'– and – some – honest – thieving –' the homily trailed off.

Eyes and medallion were in perfect harmony . . .

'Splendid . . . Splendid . . .' lilted the Master. 'Listen carefully to me . . .'

The expression on the rough, tanned face was blank. Pinpoint pupils, moving rhythmically, never deviated from the swaying stone.

'Listen only to me . . .'

Left, right . . . left, right . . . Eyes and medallion were in metronomic accord . . .

'When you wake, you will do exactly as I tell you . . .' crooned like a lullaby.

The power he could wield through hypnosis

afforded the Master great pleasure. Ascendancy, in no matter how minor a degree, tickled his vanity. His name – the Master – was symptomatic of where his desires were aimed. Some day he would become Master of the Universe . . . the Cosmos . . . meanwhile, taming this amoeba was a necessity.

'Exactly as I tell you, Sabalom . . .' The puppet must be soothed into abject obedience.

'Are you listening . . . Sabalom . . . my friend . . ?' he paused to allow for the slurred 'Ye-e-es.'

Nothing.

'Sabalom Glitz . . . are you listening . . ?' Smooth as silk . . .

'Not really,' came the bright and breezy reply. 'I was wondering how many grotzis that little bauble cost you!'

Infuriated, the Master tucked the medallion away and opted for a more direct method.

Lugging a chest from beneath the console, he threw open the heavy lid.

'Perhaps this will appeal to your crass soul!'

The chest was full to the brim with gold trinkets, gleaming silver goblets, and priceless gems.

A transformation overcame the acquisitive crook.

He could hardly breathe.

He was overwhelmed by this vision of El Dorado!

'Truly a heart-warming sight for a connoisseur such as myself.'

Now he *was* mesmerised!

Nothing could seduce his gaze.

A swarm of asteroids could be approaching and Glitz would not stir!

'There isn't a living creature I couldn't bribe with that lot!'

Bribery and corruption were the two gods whom

Sabalom Glitz worshipped. Wherever he travelled, he'd managed always to grease the palms of officialdom: civil dignitaries and senators, policemen and lawyers, presidents and dictators, all had been suborned.

The necklace of diamonds entangled with a lapis lazuli and sapphire tiara, was alone worth a cool million grotzis.

As for the ruby the size of a plover's egg . . !

'Yours . . . if you follow my orders.'

The king's ransom could have been the widow's mite for the Master! He was bidding for higher stakes.

'You're talking the language I relate to.' Glitz's paws were itching . . . aching to touch . . . to caress . . .

'Link up with the Doctor. And lead him to the Valeyard.'

Fear battled with cupidity. 'Why me? Why can't you do it?'

'He would not trust me.' It didn't take a genius to arrive at that conclusion.

'What makes you think he'd trust me?'

Like iron filings to a magnet, those rapacious digits were being lowered into the cornucopian chest.

'He's a sentimental fool. Always had a soft spot for a petty rogue!'

He slammed shut the lid – fractionally missing Glitz's hurriedly withdrawn hands!

16

Point and Counterpoint

The junior Mr Popplewick was absent.

Desk, single candle and other accoutrements of the fusty, Dickensian office were still in place. Only the diligent clerk was missing.

The Doctor poked and pried. Mel, trailing behind, was more circumspect in what was for her an antediluvian reconstruction of bygone days.

'I still reckon we'd be better off outside the Matrix,' she said.

'You do?' A hypothetical question. He was riffling through the leather-bound ledger.

'Seems to me we should try to entice the Valeyard to where the odds would be more even.'

'How do we do that?' He flipped open the lid of the desk. Empty.

'Well, since you're obviously determined to stay inside the Matrix . . .'

'Yes?'

'I hate to say this.'

'Force yourself.'

'Why don't we use you as bait.'

'Assuming it is me he's after,' responded the Doctor, jostling her into the second office.

This, too, was deserted. No senior Mr Popplewick.

'Oh come on,' continued Mel, scathingly. 'Look at the elaborate lengths he's gone to already.'

The Doctor recommenced his prying. 'Yes. They have been elaborate. Maybe too elaborate.'

Obscure remarks from the Time Lord were par for the course, but the straightforward Mel rebelled against ambiguity. 'There are occasions in our relationship when I feel an interpreter wouldn't come amiss!' She stomped to the door labelled WAITING ROOM . . .

'Don't go through there –!'

Too late!

A voracious Tyrannosaurus Rex reared towards her from the midst of a curtain of fire!

Peeping through the keyhole, Glitz saw the primeval apparition fractionally before Mel slammed shut the door.

He almost suffered a cardiac arrest!

What had he landed himself in now! When he and the Doc had gone into that waiting room, they'd ended up on the sand dunes. That was grim enough, what with the Doc sinking in the mud and then them being hounded by a cloud of asphyxiating gas! But it seemed there were nastier surprises in store!

Never keen on surprises anyway, he tiptoed across the junior Mr Popplewick's office towards the exit.

Half a mo! What about those jewels . . ? He'd stand no chance of getting them if he disobeyed orders . . .

Hesitating in mid room, he found himself level with the desk . . . Ever the opportunist, a firm advocate of 'not looking a gift horse in the mouth', he lifted the desk top.

Nestling in the previously empty desk was a black oblong box . . !

A frisson of ecstasy raised a rash of goose-pimples as he purloined the priceless cassette –

'Sticky fingers, Mister Glitz?'

The thief almost vacated his skin! Half-rimmed spectacles resting on his retroussé nose, quill pen lodged behind his left ear, Mr Popplewick senior had entered the office!

Despite the veiled threat in the steely accusation, Glitz clung onto the cassette. He read the inscription. ' "Matrix Memory Bank". I thought this was destroyed on Ravolox.' An understandable comment. He had stolen the cassette himself, only to have it snatched from his grasp in the holocaust that overtook his enterprise.

'That was a duplicate. This is the master tape.'

' "Phase Three, Four, Five, Six"!' Overawed, he hugged the cassette to his well-protected bosom. 'All the secrets of the Matrix!'

'Not all. The primitive phases one and two have been relegated to the archives.' The precise, civil servant diction was out of sync with the authoritative manner. 'Now will you kindly put it back.'

'Mr Popplewick . . . I'd give my soul for this . . .'

'You would?' Popplewick calmly extracted an old-fashioned flintlock from his frock-coat pocket. Cocked it. 'Would you indeed . . .'

His soul he may be prepared to sacrifice, his life never!

Gulping, bewitched by the barrel of the gun but still nursing the cassette, Glitz made one last bid. 'Ah, you want to negotiate, Mr Popplewick, sir . . .'

'Look at this, Mel!'

The Doctor's search had unearthed an interesting item: a scroll with a list of names.

Mel wasn't impressed. After the shock of what lay beyond the waiting-room door, she was even more anxious to quit the Matrix and return to reality.

She scanned the scroll. 'A list of names. Whose?'

'Time Lords attending my trial. Every member of the Ultimate Court of Appeal. The Supreme Guardians of

Gallifreyan Law.'

The import of the list was lost on Mel.

Not on the Doctor. Gathering these worthies to-gether for the purposes of officiating at a major trial, was to be expected. Finding their names on a scroll in a factory clerk's office, was not.

'Why're they all crossed through?'

In her inimical fashion, Mel had voiced his own query. A thick, black line was scrawled through each entry. He did not know the reason, but the vehemence with which the lines had been drawn, made him apprehensive.

So did the handwriting . . .

'Notice anything, Mel?'

She studied the document. Shook her mass of red hair.

'The handwriting.'

Sudden realisation. 'It's yours!'

Absolutely true. Each vowel, each consonant, bore the indelible curlicues of the Doctor's calligraphy.

'Did you?'

'Write it? No, Mel.'

'Then who?'

He knew who.

What he didn't know was why.

But all hypotheses were curtailed by the arrival of two visitors.

17

About-face

Popplewick and Glitz bundled into the office.

The flintlock was cocked.

But no longer by Popplewick!

The corpulent clerk flinched as Glitz, swaggeringly cock-a-hoop, jabbed the ancient weapon into Popplewick's rump.

The tables had, apparently, been turned.

'Whoa! That's far enough,' cautioned Glitz.

'I really must protest at this unseemly behaviour.' The bumbling speech pattern had regained its hint of humility. 'You are contravening all established procedure!'

'Due to my not inconsiderable powers of persuasion,' gloated Glitz, giving Popplewick's ample form another emphatic jab with the barrel of the flintlock. 'This menial's agreed to take us to his boss. The mysterious Mr J. J. Chambers, Doc.'

'Good.'

The Doctor had not finished studying the names. Nor had he been able to deduce the reason for their being crossed through. He wondered whether to ask Popplewick – then decided against bothering, convinced the explanation would not be forthcoming.

Stuffing the list into his pocket, he deliberately grasped the handle of the waiting room door. 'Will you lead the way, Mr Popplewick?'

'No!' The flabby cheeks wobbled with alarm. 'Not through there! Er – Mr Chambers is across the courtyard, sir.'

'Yeah, well if he isn't – there's going to be one bureaucrat less in the Matrix!'

With a weapon in his hand, Glitz felt very brave!

Yet . . . how did he get the weapon . . ?

Not having witnessed the earlier exchange between the pair, this was a puzzle of which the Doctor had no knowledge as the quartet filed through both offices.

He did have knowledge of another hazard though.

'Just a moment, Mr Popplewick.' He plucked the quill pen from behind Popplewick's ear and laid it delicately on the desk. 'You'll not be needing this.' When the combat of the quills had been raging in the courtyard, the Doctor was in his zombie-like state. His faculties had been anaesthetised by the disorientating onslaught to which the Master had subjected him, yet his senses – especially that deeper sixth sense – had registered the attack.

'Very astute of you, Doc,' congratulated Glitz. 'You should live long.'

'I already have. More than nine hundred years. Carry on. Carry on,' he chortled merrily.

'Get cracking!' growled Glitz, giving another jab to the clerk as he led the way through to the courtyard below.

Mel delayed. 'Doctor, what's the secret?' Mercurial changes of mood were characteristic of the Time Lord, but Mel had a feeling this flippancy was all an act.

'Secret, Mel? Secret?' He was still grinning.

Evasive responses irritated her. 'Don't patronise me, Doctor!'

'Is that what I'm doing?'

'I'm on your side, remember.'

'A stout ally.' A twinkle. 'Not a very appropriate description, eh?'

'Better than usual. At least you've not referred to me as an elephant.' A joke he made frequently.

'Because of your fantastic memory, Mel.'

She had this phenomenal capacity for total recall. Odd, really, that computer programming should be her profession since computers had virtually made memory redundant; at least, where facts and figures were concerned.

The outstanding ability intrigued the Doctor. It had also proved invaluable to him on many occasions; the most recent being when he had been battling against those Vervoids. That was when the 'elephant' joke had begun. 'Memory like an elephant' was a ludicrous comparison – the ton weight pachyderm and the featherweight girl!

'I'm not short on intuition either. And I know you know something you're not telling me.'

'Do I, Mel? I wonder.'

Gallantly gesturing her to precede him, he held open the door to the balcony.

Mel was right.

He was harbouring a secret.

At least, a suspicion.

One that involved both Mr Popplewick and the Valeyard . . .

18

Two-faced

An unseen sentinel saw the Doctor, Mel, Popplewick and Glitz descend the Fantasy Factory's stairs and troop across the yard. The matching blackness of the concealed observer's tunic, gloves, and beard, blended with the darkness shrouding the niche in which he lurked.

The Master exercised, for him, herculean restraint as he watched his eternal foe lope past well within range of the TCE . . . just one blast and an exquisite consummation of revenge would be realised. Clemency was not an ingredient of that restraint: the flintlock poking Popplewick's spine meant a greater victory was within grasp.

The fretful bureaucrat led the unsuspecting exodus to the gated entrance of a kiln: a bulbous, bell-shaped edifice that tapered into a soot-soiled chimney starkly silhouetted against the lowering night clouds.

'This is the abode of our revered Mr J. J. Chambers, sir,' announced the corpulent Popplewick.

'So he's been here all along! I've misjudged Mr J. J. Chambers alias the Valeyard.'

Alias? Chambers? Valeyard? Mel was nonplussed!

Not the Doctor. He was blithely heading into the kiln.

'Hey wait! Stop and think before you go barging in –!'

The Doctor ducked through the entrance.

'How he's managed to survive for nine hundred years beats me!' she complained, trailing after him.

The unseen sentinel now awaited the next act in the drama.

The actors remaining on stage were Glitz and Popplewick.

Glitz lowered the flintlock. 'We had an agreement, remember. I've played my part and delivered the Doctor. Now for the pay-off. The cassette.'

'My gun first, Mr Glitz.' Their clandestine arrangement, made in the office, had been followed to the letter, but Popplewick did not trust the wily Glitz!

'*After* I've got the Matrix Tape.' Glitz was also practised in the art of deception!

'That, my dear sir, was not our agreement.'

'It is now, old fruit.'

'I really cannot countenance such exoteric improbity.'

'Cut the flowery spiel, fat man, and hand over the goods!'

'Oh, very well!' With an impatient gesture, Popplewick extracted the cassette. 'But I take exception to this questioning of my integrity.'

Grabbing the cassette, Glitz returned the gun. 'Nice doing business with you, Mr Popplewick.' Then an afterthought: a venial self-justification. 'Oh, present my apologies to the Doc. Tell him I haven't sold him down the Milky Way cheaply.'

'I am sure that will be a consolation to him in his final moments,' purred the clerk.

'Can't stop. Must toddle,' chirped Glitz, moving off.

'Sabalom Glitz!' called Popplewick – then levelled the gun and fired!

A derisory click. Nothing more.

A smug smile wrinkled his victim's face. 'Safety first is my motto,' he chuckled, enjoying the embarrassment of the duped clerk.

Cockily jiggling the shot he had artfully removed . . .
he swaggered on.

'Very astute, Sabalom Glitz.' The Master quit his
hiding place. 'But this *is* loaded.'

The TCE was pointed at Glitz's stomach . . .

'What's that for? I thought there was complete trust
between us.' The blustering indignation lacked con-
viction. 'I was on my way to find you.' A lie. And the
Master knew it.

'My trust in you is in equal proportion to your trust in
me.' The TCE didn't waver.

'That's all right then, isn't it. I – er – believe you
wanted this – er – Master Time Lord, sir,' he bleated,
surrendering the cassette.

The Master took it reverently and strode away. Now
he would trumpet in his coronation: undreamed-of
power was stored within this unprepossessing box. His
double pulse rate pounded in his temples. The scope of
the dominion he could achieve reduced the destruction
of the Doctor to a piffling bagatelle; a tasty *hors d'oeuvre*
to the main course.

An apposite metaphor. At the climax of their previous encounter, outwitted by the Doctor, the Master
had been in danger of becoming the *plat du jour* of a
Tyrannosaurus Rex!

Catapulted from nineteenth-century Earth at warp
speed, he and that other renegade from Gallifrey, the
Rani, had been trapped in her TARDIS at the mercy of
the carnivorous dinosaur. A side effect of the hyper-
sonic speed – Time Spillage – triggered into staggering
growth the tiny embryo that had fallen from one of the
Rani's specimen jars.

The creature continued to enlarge in the cramped
space until, a mature monster, its neck snapped against
the ceiling.

The Rani's prosaic explanations were bombastically rejected: the Master knew it was because he was indestructible!

'A grotzi for your thoughts,' interposed Glitz.

They had reached the effigy of Queen Victoria.

Foolishly, Glitz persisted. 'You've a plan, partner?'

The toadying enquiry was contemptuously ignored: why should he – the Master – deign to humour this inferior? He glanced up at the stern, regal features looming over them; even her Imperial Majesty was a lesser being; the Empire she once ruled paled into insignificance when compared to the infinite regions that soon would be under his domination.

Then would be avenged all the humiliations he had endured.

From the paragons on Gallifrey who had shunned him.

From the High Council who had exiled him.

. . . and last, but not least, from the Doctor . . .

19

Double-faced

'Doesn't that fill you with admiration, Mel? Such crafts-
manship! Pride in every cog and piston!'

Aglow with admiration, the Doctor, elbows resting
on the burnished brass guardrail, was enraptured by a
generator that occupied prime position in the spotless,
whitewashed machine bay. Enamelled in fire-engine
red, every bearing, cog, and crankshaft was buffed to
perfection. Even the interlinked leather pulley-belts
were in pristine condition.

Exasperated by his discursiveness, Mel was tempted
to remind the Doctor that the Victorians' devoted care
of machinery had not extended to people: as the works
of the author he was so fond of quoting – Charles
Dickens – had vividly chronicled.

However, she opted for more practical consider-
ations. 'Doctor, there is another priority. The
Valeyard. Remember?'

'How could I forget?'

Mr Popplewick bustled in. He was breathing heavily.
This was only partly due to the excess weight he carried.
Much of the huffing and puffing was the residue of his
humiliating contretemps with Glitz.

It was the absence of Glitz that Mel noticed.

'Where's Glitz?' Not only was the petty crook
missing but Popplewick was no longer his prisoner.

'He decided to stay outside on guard perhaps?' In
making the suggestion, the Doctor did not look up from
the machinery. It was if he could sense Popplewick's

confusion.

'Er – yes,' replied the portly clerk grasping at the opportunistically proffered straw. 'On guard. Exactly. Yes.'

'Against what?' persisted Mel.

'Mmm?' Preoccupied. Absorbed in the engine.

'On guard against *what*?' Accusatory: why should the Doctor provide Popplewick with an excuse?

The corpulent clerk intervened politely. 'I perceive Mr Chambers is not present.'

'I'd noted that too.' The Doctor's manner was mild and inscrutable.

'I'll find him for you, sir.'

'Yes, you do that, Mr Popplewick,' he replied, curiously stressing the name.

Vaguely perplexed, Popplewick lumbered from view into an alcove.

A move that prompted a complete change of tempo in the Doctor. Quitting the generator, he began hurriedly scavenging among the tools and components littering a bench.

'If I knew what you were searching for, maybe I could help – oooh!' Mel jumped, startled by the chuntering bark of the engine which had suddenly started into life.

Unperturbed, the Doctor flung screwdrivers and bradawls aside, the clatter disguised by the noise of the engine, until he unearthed a length of cable.

'I'm most awfully sorry, sir . . .'

The Doctor whipped the cable from sight.

Fortunately, Popplewick's apology had preceded his appearance. 'I am unable to locate Mr Chambers.'

'I rather thought you might have trouble – who's that?' He pointed to an area beyond Popplewick.

Falling for the ruse, the podgy clerk automatically turned to look at the 'newcomer' – the Doctor leapt upon him, clamping his wrists behind his back!

'Don't just stand there, Mel, help me!'

She needed no second bidding to join the fray.

'Unhand me!' burbled Popplewick. 'Stop!'

Together they tied his wrists to the brass rail.

'This is preposterous! You will regret this!'

Testing the knot, the Doctor then stood before his puffing hostage.

'Mr Chambers will demand an explanation for this iniquitous – this wicked behaviour.'

'Will he, Mr Popplewick?' Again the ironic stress on the name . . .

'Indeed yes, sir. Be advised he most definitely will object!'

'Well, let's ask him, shall we?' Reaching towards the round face, the Doctor squeezed a lump of the generous cheek into his fist . . . and pulled . . .

Mel gulped . . . screeched . . .

Grotesquely, a layer of ample flesh came loose . . . the loosened flesh puckered into folds . . .

Imperviously, the Doctor yanked harder . . . the flabby features stretched . . . straggling shreds of latex lengthened . . . snapped . . . and came away . . .

Then, just as swiftly, Popplewick's brown curls were vanquished.

So were his dimpled cheeks.

His brawny double chin.

And retroussé nose.

The features now exposed were thin, oval and fine-boned. The Roman nose sported no spectacles . . the straight dark hair sported no curls . . .

Only the eyes remained the same – they expressed malignant fury . . !

'Doctor . . . what are you . . . doing . . !' Mel's quavering question died as the latex mask finally broke

102

free . . . and she was able to see the face of –
– the Valeyard . . .

20

Particles of Death

The unmasking was not finished.

The Doctor tugged at Popplewick's thick-girthed paunch. Padded waistcoat and copious frock-coat were stripped away . . . to unveil the slim, black-robed prosecutor.

'How did you . . ?' The remnants of Popplewick lay strewn on the ground at Mel's feet.

'Know?'

'That Mr Popplewick –'

'Both Mr Popplewicks, Mel.'

'Were – the Valeyard?'

'The performances were too studied to be real. We Doctors have never been able to resist a touch of the Grand Guignol.'

'You'll soon have ample scope to indulge in melo-drama.' The officious kowtowing of the spurious clerk had regressed to the conniving prosecutor's abrasive condescension.

'Really? Why?'

'Overture and beginners, please . . !'

The enigmatic rejoinder worried the Doctor. He intuitively understood the psyche of the Valeyard – to his woeful regret – and knew, therefore, that the confidence being displayed was not a façade. Something had been inaugurated by this scoundrel.

What? And when?

Quite fortuitously, Mel gave him the clue. 'I preferred him when he was Popplewick,' she declared.

Popplewick! The alcove! He'd gone into the alcove supposedly seeking the non-existent Mr J. J. Chambers!

Upbraiding himself for not keeping tabs on the stout caricature, the Doctor darted into the alcove. Its sole furnishing was an oblong cabinet: an innocent storage cupboard.

But when he looked inside, he saw no shelves stacked with harmless supplies, or any artefact available in the nineteenth century. He was greeted instead by a complex array of circuitry that incorporated transducers, anodes, and cathode tubes, all interconnected with what appeared to be a magnetic relay, a flowmeter, an ionization gauge, and a phase discriminator. Flickering digital counters and luminous neons indicated the device was energised.

'A megabyte modum!' A child of an high-tech age, Mel believed she recognised the contraption. 'But what's it for?'

'Yes, do tell us,' mocked the Valeyard. 'Disseminate the news.'

'Disseminate?' The Doctor latched onto the word. He knew the futuristic compilation had to be more than a megabyte modum, but the truth was almost beyond belief. 'A Particle Disseminator!'

'Congratulations, Doctor. If my hands were free, I'd be able to show my appreciation with appropriate applause.'

'A Particle Disseminator? What's it do?'

No response. The Doctor was oblivious to everything but his thoughts.

'It seems the other half of our persona is – un-characteristically – stunned into silence.' The Valeyard's use of the royal plural 'our' was no slip of the tongue. He embodied every conceit and arrogance the

105

six quirky Doctors were heir to.

It brought home to the present Doctor how much there was in his own temperament that he deplored. In past regenerations he had been irascible, intolerant and retaliatory – an endless list, now distilled and personified in this tormenting Valeyard.

'However, I should be happy to elucidate,' the Valeyard continued.

Mel wasn't too keen on accepting the offer, but appreciating how deeply preoccupied the Doctor was – I'm listening,' she snapped, and hoped he'd keep it simple!

'That, my misguided young woman, is the ultimate weapon. Subatomic particles: gravitons, tau-mesons – all will be completely disseminated! Now you see them. Now you don't!'

'You vain fool!' she retorted. 'Destroy us and you destroy yourself!'

Her fervour invoked a gale of laughter.

'I've met some pretty despicable people in my twenty-three years, but none comes anywhere near you!' She stormed to the Doctor, shook him from his self-recriminatory ponderings. 'Do you know why he finds the prospect of extinction such an hilarious joke?'

Accosted by guilt, the Doctor tried to shrug off the ghastly image of his own transgressions: misdemeanors great and small which translated themselves into this black-robed hyena! Laughing! Joke? Mel's pleading stung him into action. 'Sorry . . . I'm sorry . . .'

'Forget the apologies. Please concentrate on what's happening here.'

'Concentration has seldom been the Doctor's strong point. Flights of fancy into the never-never land have always offered the greater attraction of escapism,' gibed their captive.

Balefully the Doctor glared at his tormentor.

Rejoicing in his task, the Valeyard persevered with his goading. 'You see, he knows the war is lost. The armies opposing him are too formidable. I'm not alone. Ask yourself, how did I gain access to this holy-of-holies – the Matrix? Only one body has the authority to sanction the privilege. The High Council of Gallifrey! Not even this dauntless buffoon can bring down such a Goliath.' Studied commonsense took over. 'So capitulate. Greet the end gracefully.'

The resentment simmering in the Doctor abated: he could scent a false trail.

And that was a garden path he had no intention of being led up! The only flowers he'd find there were those destined for his wreath! His protagonist's verbose goading was meant to divert him.

Just as the pieces were beginning to fit!

The Valeyard's threat of dissemination was tantamount to suicide. Yet the Doctor knew the narcissistic prosecutor would not allow himself to be killed. It was irrational: hadn't the trial been contrived in order that he – the Valeyard – might plunder the Doctor's remaining lives?

Survival for him was an immutable proviso.

Then for whom was this ultimate weapon meant . . ?

Realisation dawned.

Trembling, fumbling, he extracted the document taken from Popplewick's office.

'A hit list!' He waved the list of names at Mel. 'The writing, Mel!'

'Yours, Doctor –'

'Mine – and his! Don't you see! He's made a hit list! That's why they're all crossed through!'

'But they're all in the Trial Room. And we're in the Matrix.'

107

Again Mel had given him the missing fragment of the puzzle. 'The Matrix screen!' That was to be the conveyor of death! 'Mel, get to the Trial Room! Tell them to disconnect the Matrix and evacuate the Court!'

'How –?'

'Do it! Or there'll be mass murder!'

Mel hared for the exit, lampooned by the Valeyard's taunting laughter.

Their panic afforded him renewed amusement.

So did something else.

Under cover of their absorption, he had succeeded in working loose his tethered wrists . . . .

21

The Price of Vanity

'How do I get out of the Matrix?'

This was the question Mel would have posed but for the Doctor's interruption.

She wished she had persisted. The beam of Astanneus Light had deposited her in an alley . . . Perhaps if she returned to the alley, she would find an exit there.

Weaving through the warren of slums, each a decrepit replica of the other, would have confused the average voyager. Mel was above average. At least, her memory was. It led her to the exact spot.

A fruitless mission.

No shaft descended to spirit her into the world of reality.

Then her ability for total recall came again to her aid. Remembering how the bogus Mel enticed the Doctor back to the Courtroom, she recollected that the exit was effected through the wall of an archway.

Maybe the Valeyard had been seduced by his own cleverness . . .

Maybe he had unwittingly divulged the secret of re-entry to the Trial Room . . .

Gentle snores snuffled from the benches in the Court: many of the elderly Guardians of the Law, lulled by the unscheduled interval, were dozing.

Diligently searching for a precedent, burrowing in a tome of Gallifreyan Law, the Inquisitor, too, was infected by drowsiness.

Only the guards remained alert and stiffly at attention.

'Why can't we go?' Glitz was bored with watching the vegetating Court on the Monitor in the Master's TARDIS.

'We wait.'

'For what?'

The Master did not condescend to explain. He was anticipating an event: an announcement that would set the seal on his ambitions.

'Well, look, give me my divvi and I'll vamoosh.'

'Divvi?'

'Spondooliks! The swag!' A sigh of resignation at the Master's cloddish lack of familiarity with his fraternity's slang. 'The chest of jewels! I've delivered the tape, now I'm entitled to my –'

The Master clapped his gloved hand over Glitz's mouth and concentrated on the monitor.

'My Lady! My Lady!' The plaintive cry of the Keeper rushing into the Court. 'Oh, My Lady!'

'Ah . . .' The Master grinned. 'Listen, Glitz. Remain absolutely quiet!'

The Keeper's harassed baying aroused the Time Lords and the Inquisitor from their lethargy.

'An urgent message, My Lady!' Dismayed by the devastating news he had to impart, he stammered, reluctant to be its harbinger.

'I am listening, Keeper.'

'My Lady, the High Council has been deposed.'

A gasp of incredulity from the benches.

A grunt of satisfaction from the Master. He alone had put the spark to the tinder. The damaging evidence exposing the treasonable double-dealings of the High Council to cover up the violation of the sacred Matrix by the Sleepers from Andromeda, had been recorded by the renegade and infiltrated into every VDU on Gallifrey.

In their homes, recreation centres, libraries, University, and even in the Meditative Sanctums of Astral Harmony, the Time Lords of Gallifrey had learnt of the unpardonable treachery engaged in by their elected rulers: a betrayal surreptitiously maintained for centuries.

The civil disorder brought about by his exposé, exhilarated the Master. It was a hundred percent proof nectar; intoxicating him; transporting him to a state of ecstasy never before attained; made all the sweeter by the undeniable fact that the dissolution could not have been achieved but for the self-lacerating machinations of the Doctor and his alter ego, the Valeyard.

'Insurrectionists are running amok on Gallifrey!' continued the Keeper.

'Splendid! Splendid!' burbled the Master.

He imposed his image onto the Matrix screen.

'Thank you, Keeper. That is the news I have been awaiting.'

His gloating visage filled the screen.

'Listen carefully. I have an edict to deliver.'

Subdued by the impact of the Keeper's tidings, nobody in the Courtroom demurred.

'Somewhere the Valeyard and the Doctor are engaged in their squalid duel. With luck they will kill each other . . .' He paused to consider the choice prospect.

'But that is a mere coincidental occurrence. What I have to impart is of vital importance. To each and every one of you.'

A dramatic pause. That he was invulnerable, was beyond doubt. His superiority over all other beings was unimpeachable. No small voice of caution disturbed

111

this certitude.

'Now that Gallifrey is collapsing into chaos, none of you will be needed. Your office will be abolished. Only I can impose order. I have control of the Matrix!'

He flourished the cassette.

'To disregard my commands will be to invite summary execution!'

With nonchalant hauteur, he strolled to the computer.

'Now you've purged that little lot from your system, can we get on? Load the cassette.' All this talk of abolition and executions gave Glitz the collywobbles: incredibly, he was beginning to wonder if the jewels were worth the candle!

'You really are the archetypal Philistine! Moments such as this should be savoured . . .' Ostentatiously, he loaded the cassette into the computer and switched on.

Instantly he began to shiver as if struck by palsy.

In abject horror, he shied from the computer . . . but it was as though his legs were wading through glue . . . his trembling movements were exaggeratedly sluggish . . .

'What's – wha – t's – happ – en – ing –?' Glitz, too, was affected . . . slow motion prolonged each vowel and consonant.

'A – lim-bo- at – ro – ph – i – er . . .' The Master sounded like a record player in need of winding.

'A – limbo – at – r – o – ph – i – er –?'

The drawn out question echoed hollowly around the Court. Colour was draining from the screen . . . movement lost impetus . . . then stopped . . . leaving Glitz and the Master suspended, motionless, in the dismal greyness of limbo . . .

Popplewick had substituted a Limbo Atrophier for the genuine tape.

The Valeyard had triumphed again.

22

The Keeper Vanishes

The Valeyard was anticipating more triumph.

'You are elevating futility to a fine art,' he drawled. 'There is nothing you can do to prevent the catharsis of spurious morality.'

After removing the casing of the Particle Disseminator, the Doctor was tinkering with its complex innards.

So far success had eluded him. The pulsating energy discharging from anodes zigzagged along vacuum tubes and the countdown digital clock remorselessly registered each micro second.

'If *you* could compile this monstrosity – it follows that *I* should be able to unravel it!'

With the delicacy of a brain surgeon, he inserted a wafer-thin probe into the labyrinthine circuit . . .

A splutter of static forced him to jerk away . . . but not before the tips of his fingers were singed.

Mel's guess was correct.

The archway did provide access to the Seventh Door and the sealed corridor.

Clattering up the steps, she barged into the Trial Room.

'Disconnect the Matrix!'

Already distracted by the Limbo Atrophied bodies on the screen, the Inquisitor took refuge in protocol. 'Your lack of decorum, young woman, is really beyond –'

'Forget the high-flown etiquette! Disconnect the

114

Matrix and get out of this place!'

'We cannot switch off without the Keeper. And he is not present.'

True. She had despatched him to gather the latest reports from Gallifrey.

'Then send for him! Quickly!'

'Guard –' The request was belated. Infected by the panic Mel was engendering, the guard had not waited to receive the order!

Sucking his scorched fingers, the Doctor glared at the multivolt circuit. He had no technical knowledge of Particle Disseminators – and yet, as he had intimated, if the Valeyard had constructed it . . .

Similar conclusions were badgering the Valeyard. Should the Doctor dig deep enough into his sub-conscious, he might excavate the formula . . .

Regardless of a rawness caused by the chafing, he strained at the loosened bonds.

'Stay calm . . . stay calm . . .' The Doctor lectured himself. 'Think . . . think . . .' Easier said than done. The lives of all those in the Trial Room depended on him.

Including Mel's.

For it was entirely at his instigation that she was there . . .

The petrified images of Glitz and the Master began to decompose.

'We'll have to get out!' Mel didn't understand the degenerative collapse happening on the screen, but she knew that's where the danger lay. 'If it's not already too late!'

Neither guard nor Keeper had arrived. Presumably the bearer of the Key could not be found. Or the guard

115

had panicked and fled!

'Too late . . ?'

'Get out . . ?'

'Why is she shouting . . ?'

'What shall we do . . ?'

General indecision and confusion spread.

'Unhand me, woman!' This from an elderly sage whom Mel was attempting to usher along the narrow aisle.

'Move! If you don't want that to happen to you!' She pointed at the disintegration underway on the screen.

In confirmation of her dire prediction, flowing tentacles of ions swirled from the screen and advanced into the Courtroom . . .

'The Ion Avalanche Diode! That's the clue!' The Doctor sounded far more confident than he felt. 'If I increase the particle velocity by a factor of ten . . .' he twirled a tiny ratchet –' . . . that should overload to destruction this obscenity you've devised.'

Standing clear, he waited for the de-acceleratory whine . . .

The Particle Disseminator did not even hiccup . . !

Multi-layered ghosting caused the factorising images on the screen ominously to lose definition as the build-up of ions invading the Court broadcast the malaise.

Already several Time Lords were slumped over and inert, their aged physiques unable to resist the corrosive onslaught.

Fit and young as Mel was, her legs lacked co-ordination too. In a despairing bid for safety, she attempted to reach the exit.

But every step was like walking in an ocean of treacle . . . she wasn't going to make it . . .

– then the screen imploded . . !

'Eureka!'

The Doctor pranced out of the alcove.

'So it couldn't be immobilised!'

The triumphant declaration spurred the Valeyard into straining harder at the bonds. He, above all people, recognised the Doctor's questing intelligence: had he mustered that intellectual prowess sufficiently to abort the débâcle? 'What've you done?'

'Stimulated an antiphase signal that'll nullify the Telemetry Unit. The whole system should self destruct!'

'You blundering imbecile!'

'Yes, well you would think th –'

'You've triggered a Rayphase Shift. There'll be a massive feed-back. Into *here*!'

Wrenching free, he knocked the Doctor aside and scrambled for the Particle Disseminator.

Mauve signals changed to indigo . . . to sulphurous orange . . . to palpitating gangrenous emerald . . .

'No!' protested the Valeyard, grappling with the controls. 'No, it must be aborted!'

It couldn't be. The disseminating process spewed the glittering fireflies of ions into the engine bay.

Bombarded by the ions, the Doctor, who had fetched up near the door as a result of the Valeyard's blow, managed to drag himself clear.

Not so the Valeyard.

Silhouetted by multi-layered ghosting, on his knees, he dragged his impoverished body across the floor . . .

Almost spent, with agonising slowness, his twitching fingers scrabbled for sanctuary . . .

Leaning on the gate to the kiln, the Doctor gulped air –

117

succour for his oxygen-starved blood cells.

Wanting to put distance between himself and the results of the Rayphase Shift, he staggered to mid courtyard.

The fairy lights of the Fantasy Factory were dimmed by what can best be described as a volcanic firework display above the bulbous kiln.

White, red, blue, yellow.

In torrid primary colours, the disseminating particles were shooting, in spiralling tentacles through the chimney.

Whoosh!

In a rapid succession of pyrotechnics, burst followed burst, their ferocity intensified by the tapering stack they had to mount before dispersing into the extravagance of Space: Bonfire Night and the Fourth of July condensed into one magnificent spectacle.

A twinge of sadness furrowed the Doctor's brow. He transferred his gaze to the kiln's entrance . . . the Valeyard was still trapped inside . . .

He should have been relieved.

He wasn't. Being party to the death of any living soul was anathema to this Time Lord.

Even that of a nihilist as evil as the Valeyard.

His weary tread reverberated on the cobblestones as he turned sombrely towards the archway. On the previous occasion he had taken this route, he reflected, that bogus creature had been guiding him to the spurious trial and intended tête-à-tête with Madame Guillotine.

Bogus creature!

Mel!

Was she safe?

Weariness evaporated. He pounded into the tenebrous tunnel.

118

His intended destination was a shambles.

The benches, cluttered with the inert forms of slumped Time Lords, were littered with debris.

A pall of stillness hung over the Courtroom.

Cream and red uniformed guards were in recumbent huddles beside the white-gowned Inquisitor whom they had valiantly attempted to rescue before they, too, succumbed to the disseminating ions.

But of Mel there was no sign.

Had the Doctor's retrieval come too late?

Had she, in trying to save the Time Lords, been herself struck down?

Wait! A movement from the dock.

Almost imperceptibly, a blue-clad arm flexed . . . Mel, dazed, groped for the handrail to haul herself upright.

Simultaneously, the Inquisitor stirred . . .

Nullifying the Telemetry Unit and provoking a Ray-phase Shift may have induced a massive feed-back into the kiln . . .

But it had also saved the occupants of the trial Room . . . the Supreme Guardians of Gallifreyan Law . . .

23

Carrot Juice

The Matrix screen was a gaping hole.

A vivid reminder of the fierce implosion.

'That's simply a piece of hardware. It can be repaired,' said Mel, stoically. 'At least none of us was permanently damaged.'

'For which we have you to thank, Melanie,' the Inquisitor insisted.

'Not me. The Doctor.'

Promptly on cue, the hero made his entrance.

'Now let's see, where were we? I was about to be sentenced, I believe.' The overtly contentious sally was an indication of his relief at finding Mel and the others unharmed.

The Inquisitor smiled.

'All charges are dismissed. We owe you an immense debt of gratitude.'

'Hear, hear!' applauded the Time Lords.

'In that case, we'll bid you goodbye. Come along, Mel –'

'No!' quavered a Time Lord.

'Don't leave!'

'Tell him about Gallifrey!'

'He doesn't know what's happened!'

'He must be told!'

'We may require his help!'

The overlapping protestations stopped the Doctor in his tracks.

'They came to bury Caesar, now they praise him,'

quipped the Doctor, mutilating Shakespeare's text. 'What don't I know?'

Quelling the hubbub, the Inquisitor explained.

'There had to be a reason for the Master's brooding presence,' commented the Doctor when she had related her tale.

'Doctor . . . after you learned of the High Council's transgressions, you uttered some bitter statements.'

'I don't reject them.'

'A harsh judgment.' A gentle rebuke from the Inquisitor.

'Made in haste, you consider?'

'Oh he'll repent them at leisure,' mediated Mel.

'No.' The Doctor was adamant. 'The abuse of power is repugnant to me. Discovering its existence among the elite of Gallifrey –'

'A tiny minority only, Doctor.'

Murmurs of approval for Mel's wisdom!

'Don't help her out, Mel. The honourable lady's leading somewhere, can't you see?'

'Where?'

'She wants me to go home to Gallifrey!'

'I do. Once law and order have been re-established, a new High Council will need to be elected . . . Can I persuade you to stand for President again?'

A chorus of approval from the benches.

Ever the Thespian, the Doctor gave a deep bow. 'I thank you for your confidence, my Lords, but . . . I've a better idea.'

'He's going to suggest you stand!'

Mel's adeptness in anticipating her mentor was improving.

'Indeed I am. And if there were such a thing as an intergalactic postal vote, you'd have mine!'

'I shouldn't advertise that if I were you, My Lady,'

teased Mel.

Amused by the impish banter, the Doctor ushered his companion towards the exit.

'Ah –' he paused. 'Er – there is a small favour I'd ask.'

'Name it, Doctor.'

'When you restore the Matrix, I don't care what you do with the Master . . . but apply leniency to Sabalom Glitz. He's not beyond redemption.'

'Just don't let him near the crown jewels!' advised Mel.

'Gallifrey doesn't have any crown jewels,' chuntered the Doctor as they left the Courtroom and approached the TARDIS.

'Right, a bracing glass of carrot juice . . .'

Carrot juice was a pet hate of the Doctor's! He frowned his protest.

'. . . then we'll get you on the exerciser.'

Mel's determination to reduce those excess bulging inches had not diminished!

'Perhaps I've been rash in refusing to stand for Lord President . . !'

'Come on!' The diminutive companion bundled the Doctor into the TARDIS.

'Carrot juice!' moaned the Doctor.

Later, over the bellow of the TARDIS's dematerialisation, his plaintive cry could still be heard.

'Carrot juice . . . carrot juice . . .'

Tottering on unsteady legs, the Time Lords gladly quit the Trial Room.

'Keeper!' called the Inquisitor.

Having arrived, the official stood with his back to her, gazing at the wreckage.

'Repair the Matrix screen, Keeper. Requisition any items you need.'

'Yes, My Lady.' The muted reply was deferential . . .

Gazing sideways, he watched her leave . . .

Then turned . . .

The Key of Rassilon gleamed on its silver chain, the flowing copper-coloured robes fell in folds about the spare figure . . . but the smiling face framed by the russet skull cap . . . was not that of the Keeper.

It was the Valeyard's . . .

And the sardonic laugh that resounded around the deserted Court was his too . . .

Epilogue

Mel wasn't laughing.

The Doctor had just told her they must part.

'You're from my future, Mel. You can't stay with me now.'

'So what happens?'

'For a start, I don't have to drink carrot juice!'

'No, seriously.'

'You were taken out of Time for the purposes of the Trial. Now you've got to be returned.'

'Well, can't you work a fiddle or something? Change Time and let me stay?'

'Change, Mel? Haven't I just been tried for –'

'Meddling. I know. I know . . . When?'

'When what?'

'Am I to be taken back?'

'Look at the console.'

Not a flicker of movement.

The Doctor had followed all the recognised procedures, but, except for dematerialising the TARDIS, the sophisticated mechanism was non-operative.

'We have to be placed in the exact situations we were in before we were – hijacked, so to speak. Neither you nor I have any choice, Mel.'

Despite the quiescent interior controls, the TARDIS was moving. The beam of light that had abducted the police box and wafted it to the Space Station housing the Courtroom, was now propelling it towards a destination that lay in the Doctor's future. Mel had to be restored to Oxyveguramosa, a verdant stellar fragment in the Apus Constellation. Only then could the Doctor be returned to the position in Time from which he was snatched. He wondered whether to attempt an explanation of the chronology to Mel. 'I'd better not,' he muttered.

'What?' enquired Mel.

'Oh, nothing. Nothing. Just thinking aloud.'

Before she could nail this evasion, the TARDIS jolted to a halt.

'Au revoir, Mel,' he said teasingly.

She hesitated, reluctant to leave him.

'Go on.' He empathised with her qualms. 'You'll be with me again. Quicker than you imagine. Who knows, maybe a slim-line version!'

Mel exited.

She turned back and blinked – two TARDISes in the shape of the blue police box were standing side by side!

Before she could collect her senses, one of them dematerialised . . .

Tentatively she entered the remaining Time Machine.

'Mel, you promised you'd have this programme completed!' The Doctor was tinkering with the computer . . . what's more, he had shed several centimetres from his girth!

'Cat got your tongue?' he grumbled. 'Don't you want to resume our fascinating travels?'

'That depends.'

'On what?'

'How much you've confused the situation.' She peered at the VDU. 'Move over!'

Not offended, he grinned. Having this dynamic redhead as a companion was a prospect he viewed with unqualified pleasure.

But that pleasure was to be tempered by a hazardous journey into uncharted territory.

Hazards that were destined to have a profound impact on the Sixth Doctor.

For he was about to embark upon a series of adventures that would eventually culminate in a confrontation with the Rani.

After which, this Doctor would never be the same again . . .

DOCTOR WHO

	TERRANCE DICKS	
0426114558	**Doctor Who – Abominable Snowmen**	£1.35
0426203054	**Doctor Who–Ambassadors of Death**	£1.95
0426200373	**Doctor Who – Android Invasion**	£1.25
0426201086	**Doctor Who – Androids of Tara**	£1.95
0426193423	**Doctor Who – Arc of Infinity**	£1.35
	PAUL ERIKSON	
0426202538	**Dr Who – The Ark**	£1.75
	IAN MARTER	
0426116313	**Doctor Who – Ark in Space**	£1.95
	TERRANCE DICKS	
0426201043	**Doctor Who – Armageddon Factor**	£1.50
0426112954	**Doctor Who – Auton Invasion**	£1.50
	ERIC PRINGLE	
0426201582	**Doctor Who – The Awakening**	£1.50
	JOHN LUCAROTTI	
0426195884	**Doctor Who – The Aztecs**	£1.50
	TERENCE DUDLEY	
0426202546	**Dr Who – Black Orchid**	£1.75
	DAVID FISHER	
042620123X	**Doctor Who – Creature from the Pit**	£1.95
	DAVID WHITAKER	
0426113160	**Doctor Who – Crusaders**	£1.50
	TERRANCE DICKS	
0426116747	**Doctor Who – Brain of Morbius**	£1.95
0426110250	**Doctor Who – Carnival of Monsters**	£1.50*

DOCTOR WHO

0426103261	**CHRISTOPHER H. BIDMEAD** **Doctor Who Castrovalva**	£1.50
0426199596	**TERRANCE DICKS** **Doctor Who – The Caves of** **Androzani**	£1.50
042611471X	**MALCOLM HULKE** **Doctor Who – Cave Monsters**	£1.50
0426202511	**G. DAVIS & A. BINGEMAN** **Dr Who – The Celestial** **Toymaker**	£1.60
0426117034	**TERRANCE DICKS** **Doctor Who – Claws of Axos**	£1.50
0426114981	**BRIAN HAYLES** **Doctor Who – Curse of Peladon**	£1.50
0426114639	**GERRY DAVIS** **Doctor Who – Cybermen**	£1.50
0426113322	**BARRY LETTS** **Doctor Who – Daemons**	£1.50
0426101103	**DAVID WHITAKER** **Doctor Who – Daleks**	£1.50
042611244X	**TERRANCE DICKS** **Doctor Who –** **Dalek Invasion of Earth**	£1.50
0426103807	**Doctor Who –** **Day of The Daleks**	£1.35
0426119657	**Doctor Who – Deadly Assassin**	£1.50
042620042X	**Doctor Who –** **Death to The Daleks**	£1.35
0426200969	**Doctor Who –** **Destiny of the Daleks**	£1.50